Swimming in the Ocean

also by Catherine Jenkins

poetry
blood, love & boomerangs
submerge

Swimming in the Ocean

a novel by Catherine Jenkins

INSOMNIAC PRESS

Copyright © 2002 by Catherine Jenkins

All rights reserved. No part of this publication may be reproduced, stored in a retrieval system or transmitted, in any form or by any means, without the prior written permission of the publisher or, in case of photocopying or other reprographic copying, a license from CANCOPY (Canadian Copyright Licensing Agency), 1 Yonge Street, Suite 1900, Toronto, Ontario, Canada, M5E 1E5.

Edited by Richard Almonte
Designed by Mike O'Connor
Drawings by Spencer J. Harrison

National Library of Canada Cataloguing in Publication Data

Jenkins, Catherine, 1962-
Swimming in the ocean

ISBN 1-894663-17-9

I. Title.

PS8569.E526S94 2002   C813'.54   C2002-900745-3
PR9199.3.J395S94 2002

Earlier versions of some sections of this novel were published in *blood & aphorisms* and *Room of One's Own*.

The author gratefully acknowledges the support of the Ontario Arts Council through the Writers' Reserve Program and the support of the City of Toronto through the Toronto Arts Council.

The publisher gratefully acknowledges the support of the Canada Council, the Ontario Arts Council and the Department of Canadian Heritage through the Book Publishing Industry Development Program.

Printed and bound in Canada

Insomniac Press, 192 Spadina Avenue, Suite 403,
Toronto, Ontario, Canada, M5T 2C2
www.insomniacpress.com

To the feline triumvirate
for bearing witness, providing comfort
and showing me the possibilities for joy after adversity.

Special thanks to Kathy Mac, Péter Balogh,
Mike O'Connor, Spencer J. Harrison, Richard Almonte,
Jan Barbieri, James Spyker and Stan Rogal
for expertise, input, love and encouragement.

I like being on my own better than I like anything else, but I can't give up love.

> Jeanette Winterson, *The PowerBook*

Forsan et haec olim meminisse iuvabit.
Perhaps, and at some future time, it will help to have remembered.

> Virgil, *The Aeneid*
> translation Tom Jenkins

one

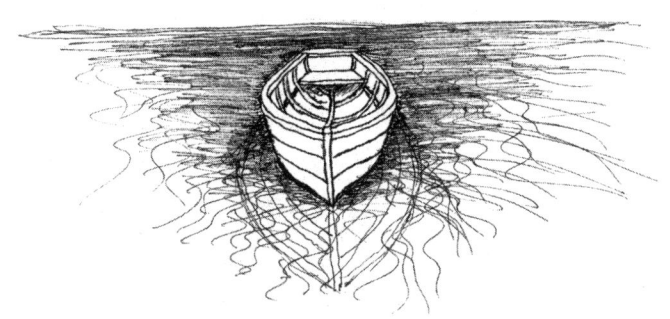

𝒜s I wait for liftoff, de-icing spray thrashes over the plane. Flecks of snow-ice thaw under pink pressurized suds. The wings are no longer white, but green.

And the thaw is upon me too, passing into feeling, freeze receding. Numbness is fleeting and now there are pins and needles. Overwhelmed, snapped back into my own reality, ice cracking off limbs and heart at the first stirrings of movement. Spring breakup hurts. Slow movement forcing blood flow past ice floes. Frostbitten. At least I *can* feel—better than amputation, losing the ability to sense anything other than phantom pain. Excruciating hurt with each thump of my heart. But I can feel something, and that's a start.

Shadows cast on the surface of the ocean by clouds seem like ghosts, echoes of lost continents adrift and drifting.

Caribbean airports always make me feel like I'm walking into a film noir. It's because they were all built in the forties and passengers still walk from small planes across open tarmac to the arrival lounge. The air, hot, thick with humidity, has a passion about it—something about the velocity of the wind in the pink-light sunset. The sign reads *Le Mirage Rest ant Bar* in violet neon. I go in for a drink, wait for a taxi in the baby blue and pink airport that's little more than an oversized bus shelter. A small yellow bird screams in the rafters as the warm evening breeze flows through the walls.

My hotel room is hot, has windows with no screens. By morning my skin is covered with bites, but the cool shower water eases the itch.

Sitting on a rock extending into the ocean gives new meaning to *alone*—an inescapable sense of it. From my beach chair, I watch time impale each wave. The smell of seaweed and bittersweet memory cascades through my blood, into my head, overwhelms. Past molecularly locked into some part of my now. Time pushes outward from its hot centre and launches me blind into the cold night of the future. Time passing to the other side of the wave, roiling back into the ocean of whitecapped water, back to a period of experiment.

    Heat...sweat...breeze...

            Pelicans...frigate birds...

                    Waves...

I'm standing on the lakeshore, smiling and faintly embarrassed. You move your arms through air, through water, in pseudo-Shiva dance style. Limbs shaking, twisting, snaking to an internal rhythm. Sweet water streaming from open-fingered cupped hands, dripping from straggly hair and goat beard. Jeans wet, eyes rolled back, you stand in the waves in your own world.

We've been smoking pot on the desolate rock of a weekday summer-cottage beach. You're relaxed; for you, twelve years my senior, smoking pot is a common occurrence. But I've been too timid, and living in too small a town, to dare approach the bad boys at school about making a purchase. The boys who talk too loudly on the school bus about acid and angel dust and speed. The boys who write me off as a good girl, who don't know my unfulfilled desires, who ignore me. Now here I am with you and we've smoked a joint. And nothing's happening. I don't feel any different.

"Here, I want to show you something." Your white dog and I trail after you to the half-completed boathouse. The structure's little more than a frame with red-stained particleboard walls. Inside, you rifle through the musty piles of precious debris that make up your life, toss artifacts to me that you think might interest—a gentleman's manicure set, X-rated Popeye comics, a collection of broken corncob pipes, rolling papers made from real hemp—before locating the roll of papers you're after. On a makeshift table you carefully unfurl pen sketches you did years ago, their detail and precision professional, almost architectural. When I ask why you aren't still drawing, you respond, "I don't want to be famous."

The sun's moving fast into the long light of dusk when your buddy calls across the water, waving a bottle of authentic mescal complete with an alcohol-inundated worm swirling loosely in the bottom. We move indoors and drink together. I'm self-conscious about my lack of experience, feel a need to excuse myself for being underage. The mescal burns like a lethal combustion of alcohol and gasoline. Mescal Sunrises and hash until early morning. Some loose combination of talk, vintage jazz and dares about who's going to swallow the worm, as I merge with the orange glow of the room. After your friend passes out and you drag him onto a bunk, we exit.

Canoeing back to your cottage, the water is clear-dark and threatening, ready to overwhelm at the least indication of disrespect. Ancient red granite boulders crevice into black water, concealing the lairs of deepwater monsters. I see bubbles of their rancid breath surfacing. I'm ever vigilant for a sudden hand breaking the stillness, grabbing my paddle. I tighten my grip and stroke faster through the pre-dawn cold.

The next morning, death seems a viable alternative. After a night of heaving undulations every time I closed my eyes, I've got the shakes. Nausea seeps through my veins. Bright sun attacks my eyes, light splits my skull. My head pulls back automatically, turtlelike, relocating somewhere behind my shoulder blades. I make myself throw up—it doesn't help. My body's defeated. Swallow hard, swallow harder. Stand still, but the sky is a moving blueness swirling into indistinct colours of light.

After a healthy breakfast of strong black coffee and granola, the world seems less volatile. Walking with you through shallow, sun-blinded water, slimy brown moss covering the rock causes me to slip, gives you an excuse to hold my hand. In that moment, I'm almost able to convince myself that I'm in love, feel a spark, an itch, an urge, a panic of desire growing uncontrollable.

We climb from the water up the steep trail to the clifftop. You assure me there's a sheer drop, nothing to smash into on the way down. My trust isn't so easily gained. I backtrack partway, drop into the water from six feet, then ten feet, fourteen, eighteen, and finally, the full twenty-two.

The fall is forever, too far to hold a breath. Inhaling and exhaling during the descent, doing a rapid-motion calculation to ensure I have air at the right moment. Water smashing into me with a cold velocity that startles breath into a submerged scream. Penetrating the water with such impact—it shatters, breaks—seems impossible it could close over me. Plunging uncontrolled deep, touching bottom, down twelve or fifteen feet to the dark rock. Trying to push upward against the intensity of the descent while I still have strength. Starving freakishly for air as I open my eyes, see the bright bubbled surface, want to escape from the cold depth. Struggle to emerge before a gasp is necessary. Crash through to light and fill with a rush of warm summer air. I climb the trail to the top of the cliff and lie in the sun, panting exhausted, proud and scared.

Granite scrapes my back as you fumble, your weight presses me into the pine-scented stone bed. Excitement overcomes you each time. At first, I'm intrigued by the texture of your cum as it lands on my belly, sparkles white as it dries in the sun. But my agitation grows with every failed attempt, the intense pressure of desire mounting to implosion. Three attempts over four days before you're finally able to contain yourself long enough to rip through my fleshy fortifications. When you finally succeed, I feel like I've entered heaven borne on wings of ecstasy, although it might only have been the effects of hyperventilation.

The blood from the wound between my legs is unstoppable. Thick, sticky blood—so much of it, I have to wear sanitary napkins. Worry that my Mother will notice, remark that it isn't time for my period. Worry she'll suggest a visit to the doctor for a checkup. Blood hemorrhages so I worry there's an internal injury beyond the simple rupturing of a hymen. Worry that there's some severe and possibly permanent damage. That I'll never stop bleeding. That I will die from blood loss caused by the loss of my virginity. Contemplate the cost of sin, despite being irreligious. Am terrified. Can tell no one.

In October, you fly to Mexico, abandon me.

I leave home, leave high school, move into a room downtown furnished with a desk, chair, bed and bureau discarded from an old hotel. The sheets and spread are faded powder blue, have seen a lot of action. A room is all I can afford and I won't be able to afford it for very long.

I feel strong, independent. I sit up late at night drinking gin and pretending I'm a 1960s New York kind of writer. I dip my pen into primary-coloured inks. Colour selection varies depending on my mood and the intention of the piece.

Then I find a used Underwood typewriter for twenty-five dollars. I light a single candle, meditate and work flow of consciousness, banging words onto paper torn from old school notebooks. I experiment with the ratio of gin to the amount and quality of written work produced. I eat cheap—not enough money to do anything else. I lose weight.

You send a single postcard, then arrive at my door unannounced late one night. You bring me a delicate medallion in an unfinished wooden box with a distinctive odour. The wooden medallion is a little larger than a quarter, lathed to fragility, hand-painted with a single red rose. There are hugs and kisses. Desire tugs deep. And then we're on the ground in Jackson's Park, hugging each other against the February wind, trying to kiss, teeth chattering. We slowly coax body parts from layers of winter clothing and howl against the wind before retreating back to my room.

Trying to understand, I challenge you. "I thought you were only interested because I was a virgin. I'm not anymore. I didn't think you'd be back." You admit my virginity was the initial attraction, but say that when you were away, you realized there was something more. And you are still the older man, the only man paying any attention to me.

My landlady doesn't like overnight guests, says your dog upsets her dog. You travel between my room, your cottage and Toronto, free-floating, restlessly looking for the path of least resistance, relying on rides, food and beds from strangers, friends, acquaintances.

We're invited to stay with a friend of yours whose house is just north of Toronto. He parks his orange jeep in the circular driveway of my rooming house just long enough to pick me up. I crawl into the cramped back seat with the dog. It's a well-used vehicle: the heater doesn't work and the metal snaps that once secured the canvas roof have corroded, allowing the fabric to flap uncontrollably in the sixty-mile-an-hour wind. In spite of the cold, I'm elated by the glowing lights of the 401 strobing orange in the clear deserted overhead night. We turn abruptly onto a secondary road overcome by an intensity of brooding dark woods, and pass a quarry pond, a deepness of black. The house rests on a rise behind that. The structure has an obvious opulence; yet between the three of us, there's little money for food.

You hone the axe as your friend grabs one of two remaining chickens from its roost and explains they've stopped laying eggs so now meat is all they're good for. The bird's eyes are dull and it puts up little resistance, barely flapping scrawny brown-feathered wings against the hand around its neck.

"You want to watch?"

I excuse myself, not wanting to watch, not wanting to hear the sound of the blade fall. Unfortunately, I can't get far enough away, daunted by the density of surrounding trees. I hear the blade strike four, five times, ringing with each effort. The axe isn't sharp enough; the chicken's neck is crushed rather than severed. Once the feathers have been removed, its carcass is emaciated, holding barely enough meat for a meal for one. The bird cooks quickly and your friend picks tentatively at its bones. I'm not hungry—I'm cold and exhausted.

I bleed that night, heavy and painful. I have to get up

several times, struggle through the unfamiliar space to the bathroom. It's one of the few nights you don't insist, commenting instead on the heat surging from my back. You hold your hand there against the cramp, a comforting closeness.

In the morning, we head into Toronto for St. Patrick's Day. The air still has a cool embrace, but it's sunny and smells of spring. We're walking along Queen Street listening to the screech and rumble of streetcars overwhelm the atmosphere, while pubs do a steady trade in green beer.

We've just crossed the street when a *screech* makes me turn back. I see a man hanging in the air for one surreal moment—then he's falling. His head hits the pavement first, then his body crumples with the impact. He's still. The city stops, inhales, is silent for a moment.

A young man steps from his car several feet away. He stands, holding the door for support. His eyes stare unseeing, face pale, unsure, translucent with shock.

A heavy, middle-aged man shatters the moment, begins to yell, "You killed my brother!" over and over. Yells with a violent urgency. "You killed my brother!" When he threatens to move toward the young man, his suddenly sober friend restrains him.

The streetcars stop. People stand watching. A man and woman from a third-storey business run across the street, say they've phoned for an ambulance and the police. You're one of the people who surround the body giving conflicting advice.

The police arrive. The driver explains quietly, "This guy just appeared in front of my car. I didn't have time to stop. It happened too fast." His fingers are a fierce white clenched against the cherry red car door. His eyes close hard against the threat of tears, his face becomes a paler grey.

Another policeman talks to the two older men who

were with the victim. "Have you been drinking?" he asks.

"We're just out celebratin' St. Patty's Day. We been to a couple a' pubs and we was just crossing to The Rex for another pint. We were just crossing the street is all."

"You didn't see the car?"

"It come outta nowhere." His eyes shift to the young driver, and straining against the hand of his friend, he yells again, "You killed my brother!"

The ambulance arrives. The victim's body is placed on a backboard with reverent care. A sheet is pulled up, but only to his shoulders. He shows some weak, uncontrolled hand movement as he's loaded into the back.

Beside me a man wearing a navy blue windbreaker watches the emergency with an open smile. I move away.

We ride back through twisting night roads to your cottage in another friend's turquoise and white '57 Ford Fairlane, vintage bebop playing all the way. He's a cabbie, a professional driver, who moves with speed and assuredness, the steering wheel gently gliding under his hand as we round each bend.

A startled glimpse of movement in the headlights is followed by a solid thump. The car slows, the two of you trying to guess what we've hit. You make him stop and then you get out alone, backtracking along the dark road. After a few more bars of Charlie Parker, you tap on the driver-side window and ask your friend to open the trunk. He turns off the ignition, grabs a garbage bag from the back seat and leaves me alone in the dark, now silent car. The only sound is your distant conversation in the black behind me. The car bounces as the trunk opens and bounces again as something heavy thumps into it. You both get back into the car.

"Biggest jackrabbit I've ever seen," you announce. Your friend restarts the car and we're off. We drive more slowly now, tentatively, round each curve straining to see beyond the glow of headlights. At your cottage, you remove the heavy bag and announce that you're going to make stew.

In the morning you're busy in the kitchen with preparations. The remaining sad small carrots and onions you grew last summer are on the cutting board. You've raided cupboards for herbs that have lost their flavour over decades of summer and winter storage. You've skinned the carcass, exposing raw muscle and bone. Guts slide onto the wooden tabletop. I'm reminded of biology class dissections and my nose is suddenly full of an imagined stench of formaldehyde. I refuse to eat your roadkill stew, surviving instead on bread and sumac jelly.

The ice on the April lake is receding from the red granite shore. On a dare, I wade in. As water climbs past my calves, numbness penetrates. I will myself further forward, past my thighs to my pelvis. An immediate paralysis sets in from the waist down. I stand, unable for a moment to do anything. I finally turn, slosh back to shore, jeans fast-freezing to my unfeeling skin.

I can't afford the room downtown through the summer so I move back home. Sometimes I borrow the car, an old blue Dodge Dart with a loose connection to the radio. Every few miles I have to slap the underside of the dashboard to make the wires reconnect. I drive through dynamite-blasted red granite valleys to visit you. The road, a complex, convoluted curvature of rock, facings turning and rising. At moments, the hood of the car overwhelms my vision before the road dips and turns to the right or left.

I usually arrive late in the afternoon and stay until early morning, almost dawn. I guess we talk but I don't remember what about. We smoke a lot of dope. Have sex three times a visit on average, ten minutes or so at a go, so we're really only having sex for half an hour—not excessive. But I find myself in tears, not knowing why. Something nagging at the back of my intuitive brain, gnawing at my belly. Somehow there's never enough time, never enough internal sweat. You spit on me to provide adequate lubrication.

And you seem to have a lot of trouble with condoms. They invariably break on impact, snap and disintegrate. I sit in the Borax stench of the outhouse, bearing down as hard as I can against your impending sperm, doubting whether gravity and shear determination will provide adequate birth control.

I leave for home half-asleep, nervously alert with the suddenness of waking. I've got that four a.m. stale metallic taste in my mouth and a dry sting in my eyes. The drive is filled with paranoia. Fear that a minor miscalculation will send the vehicle careening into a high-speed pinball ricochet, bouncing between unforgiving granite bumpers. The movement of my headlights causes shadows to shift, forming monsters in the menacing overhead trees. Their movements advance and chase me through the night. My hands tense with attention on the wheel, I concentrate hard to stay on the road. Alone in the car, in the empty dark—an ethereal isolation, disorientation. I fear it will never be morning again, that I will always and forever be winding down a formidable road. Somehow I always get home, never get pulled over, never crash.

My parents won't let me drive to Toronto, so when you and I can't get a ride, we hitchhike, usually picking the wrong time of day to leave. On the roadside I'm stationed in front to show feminine charm, the lure.

A truck passes. Brake lights flash on well past us as it commandeers the slow lane, unmoving, then starts an unsteady reverse. To prevent the foreseeable accident, you run ahead, pull open the passenger door and talk to the driver. After a moment, the truck pulls away helter-skelter into highway traffic, merges with the flow.

I'm surprised that after waiting on this busy but

unfriendly road, walking for the past two hours, you've passed up the only ride offered. You explain, "There wasn't room for both of us. He would've taken you, but I didn't think you'd want to take it by yourself. He had pelts on the floor of the cab, a dead animal in back and a rifle on the seat beside him."

It's the middle of the night in the middle of nowhere. We're still stranded on the roadside and the air's getting colder by the minute. Ahead, a crossroad is red-lit for a four-way stop. There's a closed garage on one corner and when we check the doors of the abandoned cars in its lot, we find one unlocked. We get in, you in front, me in back shivering, not sure what I'm doing here, only trailing after your aimless movements.

Morning was never so brilliant and welcome. The first ride of the day a five a.m. traveller, his car smelling of fresh coffee and heat. He produces a bag of doughnuts, the sick-sweet of icing sugar warding off the hungry cold.

Another day, a luckier day, a big-rig driver taking us most of the way. Riding up high in the cab, feeling on top of the world and vulnerable. In bumper-to-bumper traffic he lights a cone-shaped joint that takes three of us most of the two-hour journey to smoke.

"That's where I jackknifed my rig once," he confesses, pointing to an undistinguished section of the 401. "Black ice," he says in explanation. "Couldn't do a damn thing."

In the city, we stay with your friends. I don't know anybody. We flop wherever—the studio with a window onto the roof overlooking The Barracks. Your artist friend who lives here grows pot in a roof garden, sells drugs to support his art, his wife and baby. We watch body-proud men come and go from the baths, make guesses about the contents of their gym bags. The retired sea captain next door makes a sport of raining down the contents of his chamber pot on their heads, but he rarely hits his target. I'm surprised by the hostility, don't understand why you and your friends set these men apart. I observe but don't participate, am unsure what to say to make you stop.

Dusk overcomes the city and I come inside. I lie on a mattress on the floor covered by questionably dirty sheets, bathed by the light of the CN Tower. Something sounds in the room. I open my eyes and see a mouse peering from a knothole in the floorboard a foot from my face. I jump with a sharp intake of breath, frightening the mouse into sudden retreat. You come in, close the window, mutter something about not wanting to bathe in microwaves.

Another time, another friend's place, a richly decorated interior, thick blue carpeting muffling the traffic noise, false books in the library, mirrored tiles on the wall up the stairs. The bed in the master bedroom is complete with a down-filled mattress, tapestried canopy and high, dark wooden headboard graced with cherubim. In the morning, finishing nails lay where they have fallen—on the pillow beside my head. "Cupid's arrows," you say, but to me they seem more like stray bullets. We breakfast in the kitchen at a table taken from a train's dining car and then we're on our way nowhere again.

In the afternoon on the TTC bus, we sit awkwardly together, sticking to the seat. The man across the aisle stares and finally breaks the silence. "What are you doing with her? Is she your daughter?" You're immediately defensive. Part of me is annoyed at being mistaken for someone so young and part of me finds your reaction, your anger, amusing. "How old is she? You know you can get arrested?" You pull me off the bus a stop early, the man still chastising your back as we retreat. "If you're doing with her what I think you are, you'd better stop!"

The subway's even more intimidating. No landmarks,

no points of reference. I'm utterly lost and forced to cling to you. The logic of the arrangement of tunnels escapes me, threatens. In the heat of summer, two young women board the train wearing tank tops. Their bare arms are a mass of bruises and black pinpricks set against round white scars. I stare, try to figure out if they just don't care or if they're showing off, making a blatant *I don't give a fuck what you think* statement. They chat and laugh over shopping bags from clothing stores. Everything about them is quite normal, except for the marks. I can't stop staring, studying their legs, their exposed flesh, looking for more echoes, shadows, scars.

I want to understand why they've done this, what they felt at the instant of penetration that made it worthwhile. I try to imagine a needle in my right hand puncturing the thin white membrane of skin on the inside of my left arm, held stiff and straight, the hand caught between my knees for stability. Nausea churns deep in my gut. You nudge me and we get off at Queen.

Another day and we're heading home. Your friend, the one who's learning to drive, gives us a ride. When he pulls the van into the fast track at barely perceptible speed, you advise him to change to a slower lane—not an easy manoeuvre on the Don Valley Parkway, the heavy flow of five o'clock cars leaving only slim cracks between their motion. Determined, his hand carefully pushes up the turning indicator to signal his intention.

Through the back window, I see an impatient driver pull his car from behind us and begin to pass. His car now occupies the space your friend intends to pull our vehicle into.

I find myself yelling, "No! No! Don't pull over!" as loudly as I can.

The van continues a slow, graceful glide into the other lane. I'm shouting but you're not hearing me. Finally you see the car in the side-view mirror. You grab the wheel to steer the van away. Your friend, indignant at the intervention, stands on the brake, stalling us between the two lanes. Simultaneously, a squeal sounds beside us as the other car's brakes are also applied. The loosely packed debris in the back of the van shifts around and on top of me, immobilizes me for a moment, abruptly thrusts back, then everything stops.

The man driving the car rolls down his window and shouts, "Is everyone okay?" He drives away assured that we are. Your friend restarts the van. Other cars clear a path, meticulously avoid us as we steer into the slow lane.

We're sitting in a coffee shop a little further up the highway. Slumped over a coffee, I drop my head into my hand and where my fingers touch, a quick shot of pain unleashes. Just above my right ear, there's a large swollen lump. A wooden chair in the load had shifted, its leg catching me in the head. The adrenalin rush of the moment had successfully masked the injury until now. My over-anxious imagination unfolds the possibility of a more serious injury if the chair had travelled forward with greater velocity, if the leg had driven into the vulnerability of my temple.

The next morning I open my eyes to an unfamiliar room. Initially, I can't remember where I am. When I get up, I want to stretch, assess the injury. I try to move my head and can't. There's pain, flights of black in my eyes. I'm terrified, immobilized. There are tears. Detached sounds.

When I go to the doctor, the light outside's too bright. On the street, people seem to stare. The complex of nerves that travel through the spinal cord at my neck have been disrupted, jangled. They're sending disorienting shockwaves of electro-chemical panic sparking to my brain.

The injury leaves me with an urge for calmness, stability. I make an impulsive decision to go back to school, enrol at the local university. I find an apartment downtown and focus on classes and essays and books. You continue to travel, hitchhiking restlessly back and forth between my apartment, your cottage and Toronto.

It's late. I'm alone. The telephone rings and it's you.

"Did I wake you?"

"I don't know."

"I'll be coming back through on Thursday. Can I crash at your place?" And so the conversation continues until your questions and answers drift further and further apart. A field of hesitation opens between each thing you say, breathlessness.

"What's wrong?" I ask.

"Nothing," you respond, then continue talking with faltering breath, panting into the phone, words hesitant.

I ask again, "What's going on?"

"I'm jerking off. It's your voice—it does that to me."

I'm not sure how to respond. Feel strangely alone, left out.

Weeks later, when you're away again, I have a dream in which you're having sex with another woman. Someone I don't know, someone closer to your age, someone with dark brown hair. I tell you and you hesitantly admit you were having sex with an old friend that night.

Don't underestimate me: I know these things. I have a weird and accurate intuitive connection to a partner's penis, a sixth sense about where it's been. The question is whether I can admit to myself what I know. That's where the communication breaks down—somewhere in the back of my head between the unconscious and conscious minds, between what I know and what I don't want to admit. But the information's there and once I have confirmation, all I can do is nod and think, *I knew it*.

I hitchhike to the cottage with you for a weekend. Your brother and his girlfriend have come up on his motorbike and there's tension. I'm washing dishes when you and your brother come into the kitchen. You make the mistake of trying to open a casual conversation.

"I'm having some trouble with one of my molars. It hurts all the time. I haven't been to a dentist since I had that root canal six years ago. Guess I should go."

"I know a good dentist in the city who has a sliding scale," your brother suggests.

"What are you saying? That I can't afford a dentist?"

"I didn't say that, but it's true isn't it?"

Then you're yelling, "It's not fucking true! I *can* afford a dentist."

And he's yelling back, "Then why don't you just fucking go instead of whining?"

"I will. When I get back to Toronto," you retort, giving him a shove.

"Don't fucking touch me. I can flatten you if I want to."

You're reaching for the butcher knife in the draining tray.

His girlfriend appears in the doorway, grabs his arm and pulls him away. The front door slams shut and outside the motorbike kicks alive and its sound fades into the distance.

I stay quiet and still in the corner of the kitchen, waiting for the electricity to discharge. You walk into the front room. I finish washing the dishes, focusing on each tine of each fork, every inch of every plate. And I recall an earlier conversation.

When you come back into the kitchen, seemingly calm, I quietly say, "You wanted me to tell you when you were being over the top. *That* was over the top. You were talking about seeing a dentist. How can a conversation about dentistry turn into an argument?"

Fist. Hard and pain against my chest. Fist. Sudden hot-cold. I'm in space. Lost in motion. Flying. Irrational movement. Surreal. Fear. Hard stop. Head against floor. Ringing. Uncertain. A second's silent pause. Your apology just as sudden. Pathetic. Begging forgiveness. Wringing your tears in the folds of my clothes. I revert to feral strategies. Can't let you see me cry, watch me bleed, show any signs of fear, weakness, paralysis. Can't leave you that opening, allow you to pounce, go for the throat. I get up slowly. Make stiff movements away from you. A strange control in the midst of shock and fragility. Anger takes me out the door to the lakeshore. I release tears quietly, my back to the window, knowing you're watching.

I should leave. But somehow can't. Feel a naïve obligation to stay and help you untangle your pain. You keep falling and I catch your weight, recognizing with slow terror that now we are both tumbling downward.

After that encounter, the venomous threats start. You say you want to tie me up, scarify me, shave my head while I'm sleeping, body vulnerable. My sleep becomes violent, erratic. I can't close my eyes until your breathing slows and evens. I feel myself literally falling into sleep and wake with a start before impact. I wake up in the night, in the panic dark, eyes wide, breath rapid, sweating. I grind my teeth to wake the dead. In the morning my mouth tastes of bitter blood and I'm exhausted. I'm losing the strength to hold you up, fight back. Losing me.

I run into an old friend. Both of us are caught in situations we need to escape but I'm too weak and past knowing how. "You don't have to stay with him," he says, and I'm not sure that had occurred to me. He and I kiss on the steps of the courthouse and I recognize a joy I'd forgotten existed.

You and I are in the living room of my apartment sitting beside each other on the couch. "I don't think we should see each other anymore." I speak very softly, frightened that the presence of these words will stimulate your rage. A pause, a gathering electrical charge. Your fists come down in unison, attack the coffee table, split it in two. Eyes wide, not breathing, I wait for your hand to make contact, but it doesn't. Instead, there are tears. Then I'm beside you, crying too.

In desperation, you say, "All my friends have betrayed me. My friends here, my friends in Toronto and now you. You're all abandoning me." Even in the midst of difficult emotion, I refuse your guilt, recognize you've created the problems you blame others for. Everyone's tired of carrying your weight. I feel strangely justified.

After more tears, rage and anger, you leave. In a mild state of shock, shivering, I lie down, huddle under blankets against an internal chill. I no longer recognize myself. You've taken more than I could give you, have left me decimated. I have to blindly relocate the pieces, rebuild the structure of myself, remake it stronger, indestructible. Start at ground zero, before impact. Try to remember who I had been, what things had defined me to myself.

I spend intimate time with my old friend. We comfort each other through our losses.

Alone in the night I repeatedly play "You Can't Always Get What You Want." Although I'm not sure what I want, I know it isn't you. Slowly, slowly rediscover myself in Van Morrison's "And the Healing Has Begun." And the small-town radio never figured out it was me phoning late at night requesting "Walk on the Wild Side" with its deceptively easy convolutions.

But the relationship doesn't end there. There's a knock at my door and it's you. Late in the afternoon, you ask to store some of your things, say you'll pick them up later. Or you present me with the biggest cucumber I've ever seen and say, "Go fuck yourself," and I'm not sure whether to laugh or be frightened. Or you ask to come in to use the telephone, then you refuse to leave.

There's a knock at my door and it's you. Evening or nighttime, too late to hitchhike out to the cottage beyond the red granite valleys, you ask if you can spend the night. I say, "No." You say, "What do I have to do? Beg?" and drop to your knees. Disgusted, unsure what to do, I let you sleep on the couch and I close my bedroom door, wishing it had a lock.

There's a knock at my door and it's you. I've decided you're not staying another night. I refuse to let you in. But you won't leave. You're not listening. Then you're inside, the door closing behind you. "Get the fuck out of my apartment!" I'm yelling. And you're still not listening. I need you to leave. My frustration and anger make me big, swell my body. I need you to leave and I'm broadcasting it as loudly and clearly as I know how to, and you're *still* not listening.

Then there it is again—fists hard against my chest.

And I'm in motion. Sudden, irrational. I fucking explode. Strike erratically. Hitting your body. Surreal. Certain. Hitting. Hitting. Feral. Cornered. You collapse on the floor, arms raised in self-defense. I make myself stop. A strange control. I scare myself. You leave.

The telephone rings and it's you wanting to come up. I say, "No." You ask if anyone's with me. I'm unable to lie. I tell you my friend's here. Then you're yelling in the night at the back of the building. In a fit of juvenile hysteria you're calling him out for a fight. Wanting you to shut up before the neighbours call the cops, I descend the back stairway to the spotlit parking lot.

"What do you want?" I ask, trying to stay sane and calm.

"I want to fight him for you."

"It doesn't work that way. I don't want to be with you.

All I want is some peace. Just leave me alone." Violence creeps up my throat, rests, sharpens its teeth, ready to launch and kill. And again you don't listen. Violence ruptures my skin. I picture my hands gripping your throat, ripping at your face. Sure at this moment I could kill you.

Fear holds me back. I pull the violence in, redirect it against myself. Take four steps back to the gold-coloured brick wall. Stand, legs solidly braced, inhale sharply and strike. Imagine the back of my head leaving a dull, crumbling impression in the brick as I impact over and over. I keep my eyes open, watch you accusingly, say, "See what you do to me?" when I'm finished.

The telephone rings and it's you. With venom, you say, "I'm going to climb to the roof of your building and watch you having sex with him through the skylight. Just before you cum, I'm going to leap through the glass and land on both of you." I hang up and walk to the bedroom. Looking up, I see the vulnerability, envision you tumbling through, showering the entwined us with shards of falling glass.

I tell him about your plan. "How did you get involved with such a psycho?" he asks, and I have nothing to say. He offers to stay the night just in case. Nothing happens. A hollow, if not inventive, threat.

Days later, I see you across the street. My breath accelerates wildly, heart in throat pumping loudly. Shakes, sweat, almost hysteria. Too scared of what either of us might do, I opt for flight. Panic every time I see you, until the last time. And then I don't see you any more.

You phoned me on my thirtieth birthday—weird and scary. I came home to find a message from you. I was frightened that you'd remembered the correct date, the correct year. In an anxious moment I looked out my apartment window for you. For three days I kept expecting you to appear, kept a twist of fear caught in the pit of my stomach. You didn't arrive. I'm not sure how I would have reacted. I've developed an extreme ability for retaining a cool exterior, even under duress, but I'd probably still have nightmares about you crashing through my front windows. Part of me wants to believe it was a sincere birthday wish, that you just wanted me to know you'd remembered. Part of me thinks you were mocking the fact of my aging, the irreversibility of time. I'm living in a different city now and hope you don't find me on my fortieth.

Frightening the damage people can do to each other without even trying. I have to give you credit for helping me find and surpass my limits; for pushing me over the boundaries so I learned their contours intuitively; for helping me slice through my emotions on a razor's edge of instability. The recovery was by slow degrees—it took years. As each element was untangled and resolved, I'd repeat, *Now I am whole again,* the sentence always ending with a tacit question mark. Another shock to the system almost ten years later finally allowed me to recover all the pieces, find their correct locations, test their stability—open the windows again.

I'm older now than you were at that time. I understand desire, at least better than I did. I can sympathize with the attraction, the appeal of youthful flesh, but I can also find a young body aesthetically pleasing without needing to possess it, to take advantage of inexperience. It seems unlikely to me that someone as young as I was would keep me interested for long, or have the emotional stability necessary for a lasting relationship. I don't enter into these forays. I'm certain someone would get hurt—quite possibly me.

I know I hurt you. I didn't intend to. I have no apology. I'm not usually so callous.

The smell of my gently heated skin in the sun, a light, sweet, natural scent. Inhaling my warmed self. The unique softness of the skin of the areola or the skin of the glans, almost too delicate, too fragile to survive; almost too thin to retain fluid inside its translucence. Contemplate the difficulties of the human body and emotion. A critical distance is necessary to converge on my emotional state.

In this place, salt pervades skin, water and wood. Land ends and utility poles anchor in the ocean, offering a stern contrast: the horizontal lines of weathered water and smoothed rock against the spindly verticals of poles and masts.

Every sound is distant and precise—a radio, running water, a clock, birds feeding—no background *huuuh* of traffic and too many people. Each sound is exact, like Arvo Pärt's "Spiegel im Spiegel;" spare piano with cello, something lovely, clear and distinct. The sharpness of the air, overpowered by waves, frightening and invigorating, encourages me to bow down and be taken. But I'm not ready yet.

In that ocean there are over two hundred species of jellyfish, a complex, translucent, jellylike community formed from many simple, connected, individual creatures. The composition of jellyfish is ninety-seven percent water; they have no gills, eyes, blood, heart or brain.

The Portuguese man-of-war is one subspecies that can sometimes be seen in swarms of thousands. A distinguishing feature of this type of jellyfish is its pink-purple-blue bladder that floats above the water and acts as a sail, allowing passive movement. Beneath the float, the creature is actually a colony of three different types of single-celled polyps, from which hang tentacles so long that even in clear Caribbean waters their tips can't be seen as they fade into the blue. The dactylozooid polyps bear harpoonlike barbs that discharge on contact, shooting into prey within milliseconds, delivering a dose of paralyzing neurotoxin. A second set of polyps acts to secure the prey and the whole jellyfish then spreads over its stunned captive, secreting digestive enzymes and allowing nourishment to circulate through the colony.

The third set of polyps deals with reproduction. An individual man-of-war is comprised of numerous asexual organisms. However, each man-of-war also has ovaries or testes, which release gametes into the animal's mouth. The male releases sperm from its mouth into the water, which the female captures in her mouth to fertilize the eggs before releasing them into the water. Many species of jellyfish proceed through four distinct phases of development. During the immobile polyp stage, reproduction can only occur through asexual budding; only when individuals reach the mature, tentacled, medusa stage, breaking away from the polyp colony to swim freely, can they reproduce sexually. Unlike most jellyfish, in man-of-wars the distinction between polyp and medusa stages is not fully made.

The complex poison from a man-of-war is seventy-five percent as powerful as the venom of a cobra. Stings to swimmers are potentially fatal, with symptoms including fever, shock and cardio-respiratory interference. The poison, which can cause continued outbreaks for weeks, causes the victim's body to release histamines. Contact also leaves red, whiplike welts or lesions that can last from minutes to hours, or ulcerate and last even longer. The most poisonous jellyfish is the Australian box jelly whose venom is even more abrupt than that of a cobra and can be fatal in less than five minutes.

Despite the dangers of jellyfish, the tiny clownfish commonly dwells in the tentacles and has developed a mucous covering that protects it from jellyfish stings.

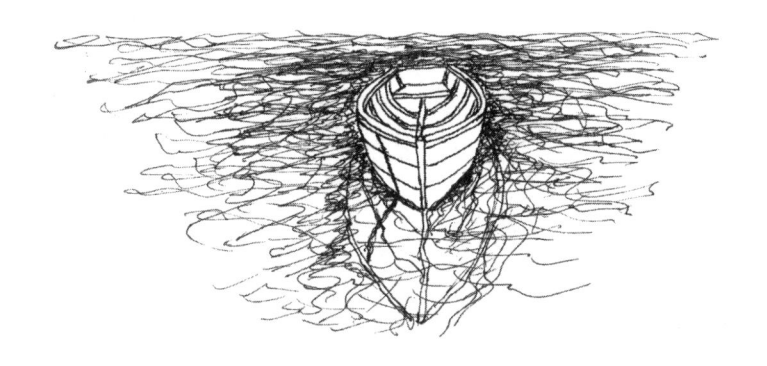

two

𝓘 move into another apartment—one without a skylight. I get a kitten, runty small and sleek black, with eyes changeable from yellow to green.

You're very different from the last "you." You're taking philosophy classes even though your major is biochemistry. We drink lots of coffee together and have after-class chats. You have an elegant subtlety to your touch, a care and precision in the way you roll a cigarette. We exchange gentle glances across a table, conversation warms your voice, triggers a glow in my waiting body—a slow build to intimacy, and finally, just the two of us in your room. Sharing the ritual undressing, I notice your shyness, difficulty at being naked in front of me—strange in my limited experience of men who are usually so aggressively in control of both our bodies. In quiet embarrassment you find it necessary to inform me that this is your first time. I inadvertently laugh, not at you (carefully, but ineffectually, I assure you that I'm not laughing at you), but at your assumption that I'm so much more experienced, that I have the expertise to ease you through this awkward moment.

You're a careful and sensitive lover, playing on the edges of Tantric, riding on the verge seemingly forever, finally spilling into mutual ecstasy. The sharing of touch as deep as internal organs, as soul. Your wonderful long fingers gentle and strong, gliding over my shoulders, over my back, through my body, slow and synchronous.

It's winter and the deep snow leaves a cold layer of white on the dramatically posed black statues of the war memorial. The smoothed red granite book of the dead lies open to a blank page, numbed by a thin layer of ice. But the sun is bright, even warm. There's joy in each step as I shortcut through the park on my way to your house.

Anticipating the wonderful, I'm not disappointed. Afterwards, I continue up George Street, elated, light-headed, sure that everyone who sees me is aware of the damp aftermath between my legs. In class, I'm distracted, have a goofy grin plastered to my face. My thoughts are where I can still feel you. On my way home in the evening, I stop in again.

You invite me to join you for some magic on the bridge after dark. You've absconded with a tiny sample of some volatile substance that explodes on contact with water. High above the current, you loosen the lid of the container holding the inert matter, then drop it into the river. For a brief moment, water penetrates the sample and it glows angry orange before sinking to the bottom. You seem a little disappointed and reticent to indulge in the experiment again with a larger sample.

I don't know how many gallons of sake you made. Drinking warm homemade rice wine in the kitchen of your house, four or five of us in chairs around the table, sipping slowly from large tumblers, growing giddy and then silent. My head lolls on my neck as my eyes lose focus. The drink, verging on hallucinogenic, is perhaps slightly toxic. By the time we've worked our way through about half the batch in several sittings, my body's had enough, my stomach revolting at the merest whiff of the stuff warming on the stove.

We're in Ottawa at Christmastime visiting your parents. The white lights of Rideau Street sparkle in the winter air as we walk hand in hand. Crossing a street, you ask the question I'm thinking of asking. "Do you want to live together?" We both know it feels right, are on top of the world with joy.

In the spring we move into our apartment, an enormous two-bedroom. There's dark wood trim throughout and lots of windows with sills wide enough for the cat to walk tightrope on. In the huge kitchen I preserve peaches and you cook better than I know how to. I watch you through neon tetras flashing blue and orange in the fishbowl between us as we work at opposite ends of the big table in the dining room. There's bright southern light in the daytime and at night the halogen spotlights of the baseball diamond across the river light up the interior almost as clearly.

Between the walls and floor and ceiling there are large open cracks. Parts of the foundation are crumbling and the various planes of the building are separating, losing the precision of their original geometry. The gaps are large enough for bats to slip through.

In the morning you're shouting me awake from the far end of the apartment. I stumble to the bedroom door and see you, wearing socks only, holding a tennis racket in one hand and a folded newspaper in the other. A bat is doing fine figure eights around the living room. When it finally settles in an upper corner, I'm the brave one who mounts a chair, towel in hand. My idea is to capture the flying rodent in the towel and toss it outside into the day, but the bat has other ideas. I'm on the chair, approaching with the towel. When I'm within a few inches, the bat, sensing my presence, takes evasive action. A projectile with beady black eyes and tiny sharp teeth launches itself at my face with a screaming squeak. I will not be so brave in future. Eventually, the bat swoops too close to the floor and the black cat knocks it out of the air. Once the bat's stunned, we collect it, deposit it on the windowsill and wait for it to leave, which it eventually does when we're not looking.

Friday night, two a.m., we're woken by a *squeak, squeak, flap, flap, flap* sound in the living room. We wait for the cat to down his prey. There's been a bit of a battle: the bat has a torn wing and the bloody indentations of teeth marks on its body, and there's a wet spot on the cat's head. I'm not sure what's happened, if there's been an exchange of body fluids. Knowing bats are potential carriers of rabies, I phone the vet; the answering service wakes him, I explain my concern. He advises me to kill the bat and take it to the Ministry of Agriculture for analysis, just to be sure.

By three-thirty a.m. we've captured the flapping, damaged bat in an overturned bucket and are psyching ourselves up for the task at hand. You carefully, meditatively, roll and smoke a cigarette. At four a.m. we're drowning a bat in the kitchen sink.

Saturday night, three-twenty a.m., again we're woken by a *squeak, squeak, flap, flap, flap* sound in the living room. Initially, half-awake, I'm convinced we're being haunted for murdering an innocent bat in the kitchen sink. I look into the living room expecting to see an ethereal white phantom doing figure eights. I'm relieved that the cat has already downed his prey. We capture bat number two in a bucket. By four-thirty a.m. we're drowning another bat in the kitchen sink. We're acquiring an efficient technique for this activity.

A drowned bat is a pathetic sight: its body is fragile and small, the thin membranous wings create a crumpled translucent cadaver. We now have two icy drowned bats in a Drum tobacco tin in our freezer.

Monday morning I take the tin and its contents to the Ministry. The man in the office is not cooperative, doesn't believe there's any possibility these bats could be rabid. At my insistence, the bats are transported to a lab where they are decapitated and have their tiny brains analyzed for traces of the raging debility of rabies. Three weeks later, we receive a notice that the bats were not rabid, everything's fine—which is good considering the brief incubation period for the disease.

There's no way to bring back the dead bats, and now that we know they weren't rabid, I feel guilty for killing them. Somewhere in the back of my head I label myself a bat murderer. We try to discourage bats from entering the apartment, but when they do, we now assume they're not rabid and just encourage them to leave.

I take a long weekend by myself at the cottage in the fall, just for a change, for a silence. The leaves are falling already; the ground is scattered with their sound. I stay up late reading—not a horror story exactly, but a story that's too possible, too potentially real, unsettling. At two a.m. I turn out the light. Outside there are sounds. I keep telling myself it's only chipmunks or raccoons, their feet rustling in the death of leaves. But part of me knows it's a large man, wearing heavy boots, carrying an axe, murder in his eyes. I can't sleep. Panic. Tell myself I'm behaving irrationally. At five a.m. I grab the cat and my bag, run out the back door to the car and escape home to find comfort with you in the dawn.

It's almost New Year's. We've each celebrated Christmas with our families and now we're together in Ottawa. I'm sleeping upstairs in your childhood bedroom while you're relegated to the rec room. Between us lie your sleeping parents who know we're living together, know we're intimate, but forbid any such behaviour in their house—after all, we're not married.

You and I haven't seen each other for five whole days. The strain of desire is intolerable. I can't sleep knowing you're so close, yet inaccessible. I fantasize about sneaking down the hall past your parent's snoring bedroom, but can't get up the nerve.

The next afternoon your father is leaving to pick up your mother from the hairdresser's. He keeps repeating phrases like, "I'll be back in a few minutes" and "We'll be right back" and "I'll only be gone for a bit." We don't even consider having sex—it would be far too obvious.

That evening, your parents entertain guests. Your mother, concerned by your father's level of alcohol consumption, removes the bottles from the counter, replacing them in the upper cupboard when she decides he's had enough. We meet the guests, then we're excused.

Your parents, perhaps forgetting that we aren't quite kids any more, send us to the rec room to entertain ourselves, watch TV or something. We fall into each other, make love as intense and silent as any covert operation. Then we take great care to rearrange the slipcover, straighten clothing over glassy-eyed stares, smooth down hair, settle our breaths before mounting the stairs to rejoin the grown-ups.

The next night at your sister's we share a wide bed as old as an heirloom. We make love, loud and intense, filling the dusty air with our sounds of jubilation and relief.

After a year in our apartment, the frost in the freezer has grown so thick that opening the door entails breaking an ice seal. The antiquated refrigerator squats in the corner of the kitchen, taking up an inordinate amount of space given its interior dimensions. You decide it's time to defrost, but not wanting to wait the old-fashioned way, you retrieve a hammer and screwdriver from the tool box. Alerted by the banging, I come into the kitchen.

I'm watching over your shoulder when the end of the screwdriver pierces the coolant coil and the kitchen is filled with vapours reminiscent of a World War I trench. We retreat, eyes burning, throats tight and, not knowing what you've just released, you decide to call the fire department. Sirens announce their arrival and large men wearing buglike masks intrude.

Only then do you remember the marijuana plant growing on the windowsill beside the fridge and realize that inviting authorities of any sort into the apartment while growing something illegal is probably not a great idea. A fireman tells us we have an ammonia leak in our fridge, advises us to try not to breathe it, to air out the kitchen well and to get a new fridge. The landlord is not happy and you never suggest defrosting a fridge again. The pot plant doesn't survive being gassed.

By summer we're living at my family's cottage, me finishing school, you applying for jobs in Ottawa where we're moving in the fall. You take several trips for interviews and job searches, leaving me alone in the woods.

Dusk is coming on and the single channel on the black and white TV is showing a horror movie. It's a hot night so I have the heavy wooden door open, the screen door closed to minimize the bug invasion. The movie becomes more intense, edgy, as the sky darkens to night. During a commercial break, I notice the small black cat transfixed, staring out the screen door. He often stares into space, seeing things beyond my ability. I promise myself that if he's still there during the next commercial break, I'll take a look.

I watch the next segment of the movie, distracted by what could be real horror outside, only a few feet away. At a high point, the station goes to commercial. The cat's still staring out the door. Nervous, high-pitched, I grab my flashlight and pick up the fire poker as a weapon. I take a few deep breaths and gingerly walk to the door. I suddenly turn on my flashlight, startling the unblinking eight-eyed intruder staring at me, low to the ground, unmoving. The cat is having a staring match with four young raccoons, more curious than threatening. After a few more moments of sizing each other up, the large mother raccoon clucks a few times, calling her children to her. Reluctantly they turn away, stop, look back, then trot after her into the forest night.

Classes take me back and forth from the woods to downtown, an almost daily forty-minute drive. There are limited choices of routes I can take, so I opt for the quickest, but it becomes a boring effort. I start to drive faster and faster, just to get it over with. On the straightaway a van pulls out in front of me at a snail's pace. When I try to pass, he accelerates to match my speed. Frustrated, I slow to pull back in behind him, but he slows too. Determined now to pass the bastard, I accelerate hard. He matches my speed and we're drag racing on flat straight road on a brilliant summer's day. Then I notice a farmer's car coming along a laneway signalling to turn into me. I radically overreact. Knowing I have to pull in behind the van, I jam the brakes, lock the wheels and go into a high-speed skid. Automatically I steer into it, but that doesn't help. Out of control but slowing, I finally land on the shoulder angling toward the deep dry ditch, having done a full one-eighty. The engine stalls. Dust almost chokes me as I collect my wits and then drive the rest of the route home at a leisurely pace. I like driving. I'm a good driver. I just don't commute well.

Each day after class I stop by the post office to pick up mail. Suddenly you're receiving two or three letters a week from a woman in Ottawa whose name I don't recognize. I consider losing your mail, burying it, but instead I deliver the letters into your hands, trying to stay calm, but needing answers. You say you met her on the bus, she's just a friend, you don't want to discuss it. Later, another friend of yours tells me the story of this woman falling asleep on your shoulder on the long ride, the scent of her hair against your cheek. And it was just too easy.

I push you for answers because this new relationship may impact my future too. At the end of the summer, you inform me that I'm not welcome, I'm not moving to Ottawa with you. A thickness of tension, tears and anger as the truck pulls away with your boxes, mine abandoned in the corner.

I'm completely lost, don't know what to do. So I stay in school, start another degree, find the only place I can in the fall in a university town on short notice. It's a dark, cold, north-facing, lonely apartment. I set up the stereo and listen to "Bed's Too Big Without You" in tears. I try to convince myself with John Waite's "Missing You." Every move, every breath, requires too much effort. I listen in the living room, in the dark, while trying not to hear the neighbours' raised voices.

The ocean is like a dark Dali. No wind today but the water's surface bobs like water in a bathtub after the fat lady has lain down. Small whitecaps create worry lines across the ocean's watery brow. Almost reflective, reflexive.

Just before a wave falls, folds over on itself, the water turns to slow-motion black, then comes up tropical green blue and frothy white, sun-glinted and blind. Its sound, the intermittent applause of trillions of droplets of water falling in a hesitant barrage.

The ocean slips onto land, invades its jurisdiction,

thrusts legs of wet vegetation onto rock. The ocean trickles and flinches against the land, teases, licks at it like a small pet. The land suffers at the hands of the ocean, yet still embraces it. The land allows its surface to be smoothed for a better fit, allows shallows to be gouged so it can retain a tiny fraction of ocean once the water retreats, abandons. These small silent waves, puddles, flat like rays.

Rays are distinguishable by their flat disc-shaped bodies, smooth skins and elegant capes of winglike pectoral fins they use to move like dark shadows through the ocean. Most have no discernible head, their eyes protruding slightly from the flat top of their body, mouth and gill slits located on the bottom. Their undersurface is always white while the upper surface is dark, ranging from almost black to shades of brown, grey or green. Their boneless, cartilaginous skeletons allow for enormous flexibility and manoeuvrability. Rays tend to be surface swimmers and will even breach water, flying through the air for several seconds.

The majority of rays inhabit shallow to mid-waters, hunting in seagrass beds or lagoons. Some rays use their unique body shape to herd plankton or small fish into their mouths, or they will suddenly lift the central portion of their bodies, creating a suction that draws prey toward them. The manta ray, which can have a twenty-foot finspan, feeds mostly on plankton in the open ocean. The electric ray is able to stun its prey with current from specialized organs, a technique that enables it to capture more active fish, such as eel, salmon and flounder. Stingrays and bat rays feed on abalone, snails, crab and conch, which they grind with the hard plates of their mouths.

The stingray has highly developed electro-receptors and acute senses of smell and touch that help in prey location. The ray covers its prey with its body, cloaklike, and buries itself in the sand to eat, leaving only its eyes showing. Although its aim is poor when swimming, the stingray causes more serious stings than any other marine creature. This is due to its habit of remaining buried in the sand during the day where any unsuspecting swimmer can easily step on it. When this happens, its whiplike tail will lash up in self-defence, the serrated spines cutting and tearing flesh, introducing a poison of unknown chemistry that, although not life-threatening, is extremely painful and can depress respiration.

Although rays usually travel alone, they have also been seen in schools of thousands, especially during mating season. In these mating herds, females may lie on top of each other, protecting those who have already mated or are sexually immature and making it clearer to the males which females are available. The male glides under the selected female with his belly to her belly, then inserts a clasper into her cloaca. While mating, the couple swims with synchronous, slow-winged strokes.

Gestation lasts eight to twelve months, with two to ten pups per litter, depending on the subspecies. Birth takes place in protected shallow bays where food is more readily available. In stinging varieties, pups are born with their tail stinger in a sheath, which is shed immediately. At birth the pups resemble a folded newspaper, their wings encasing them, angel-like, protective.

three

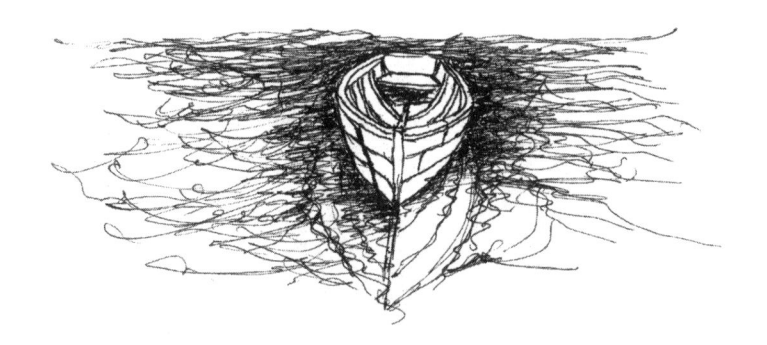

I move again. Here, the suspended ceiling amputates the curvature at the top of the old windows. The walls are covered with cheap wood panelling and the floor is covered with moss green indoor-outdoor carpeting. I feel like I'm living on a pool table or in my parent's rec room, even though I'm on a third floor downtown.

I meet you at an underground bar. You're not a complete stranger. Someone I've noticed. I take you back to my place. We have sex. It's okay. Not great. The fumbling awkwardness of unfamiliar bodies trying to be intimate. I roll over, feel a strange push-pull. Want you. Want you gone. Something. Don't see you again. I don't remember your name or even what you looked like.

I meet you at an underground bar. You look interesting. We make eye contact. You saunter to the empty chair opposite me, a glass of draft in your hand. There isn't any real conversation. I let you take me back to your place. We fuck. Wild and ruthless. I'm too tired to get home. In the morning, you've vacated. I leave. Next time I see you, you're with someone else and I don't understand the attraction. I only ever knew your first name and now that's gone too.

Someone's whistling on the street outside my window. I look. It's a young man standing in the shelter of the doorway to The Solid Rock evangelical centre. He sees me, pulls down his track pants and points to his erection like an offering. I stay away from the window but can still hear him whistling out there two hours later. I call the cops, but by the time they arrive, he's left.

The next morning, I hear him whistling again. This time the cops come immediately and arrest him for indecent exposure. After they get him to the station, they call me back and tell me about the three outstanding warrants against him: two for attempted sexual assault, one for a more successful sexual assault.

I meet you at an underground bar. You're almost a stranger. Someone I'm not sure I've seen before. I take you back to my place. We have awkward sex. I don't see you again, don't remember your name or even what you looked like.

I meet you in class. It's hard not to notice you. You strain to use big words but often do so incorrectly. Pretentious, but trying so hard for acceptance and approval. I'm not interested but am civil. You get the wrong idea. You start calling, coming to my apartment unannounced, following me around town, leaving flowers I refuse to bring inside. But you don't take the hint. I tell you bluntly that I'm not interested, feel relieved that I've gotten through. But on leaving you turn and ask, "Can I kiss you now?" You insist that *I'm* the one who's unstable, that I need your help. I experience a growing frustration and fear and have to admit I can't handle this situation by myself. You don't leave me alone until, at my Mother's insistence, the lawyers and police get involved. I remember your name, sort of what you looked like. Wish I didn't.

I meet you at an underground bar. I've never noticed you before. You take me back to your place. We fuck. It's not great. In the morning there's that awkwardness making me wish I'd found my way home the night before. I don't want to see you again. You keep calling. I unplug the phone. Forget your name.

I don't meet you at an underground bar. You're not a complete stranger. The attraction is mutual but unbalanced. We keep company but my emotion, my desire is greater than yours, makes us awkward. I'm in love. You're—noncommittal, drive me crazy. You've just broken up with a long-term partner and have started seeing someone else; you make it clear there's no room for me in this equation. But we share time and touch and almost sex, listen to reggae and smoke a lot of strong Jamaican ganja. All those times when I asked if I could stay on your couch watching the sun stream in, it was only partly because I enjoyed your company, your space—mostly it was sheer disability.

The levels of THC in my system reach a point of constant high. I have physical hallucinations even when I'm not smoking. I reach for the door handle of the car and think I've missed, think I've fallen short of my intended goal. I look down for visual clarification and find my hand *is* actually resting on the cold, smooth metal, even though I can't feel it. When I slam the door shut, for a moment I'm sure I've caught my fingers, but when I look, they're fine.

You make Duncan Hines double fudge ganja brownies. During the opening credits of *Dr. Strangelove* I find I've lost all motor control—can't move, can't talk, am scared and desperately need out of the theatre. With a concentrated effort, I finally manage to lift a hand to your arm, make some fuzzy words and you help me up. I don't remember leaving. I do remember the cold night air and throwing up by the snow fence in the parking lot.

You didn't take advantage of my emotional state. I was in love; it didn't make sense. I licked my wounds listening to Marley's "Is this Love" on the album you bought me. Still remember your name, the timbre of your voice, the lingering smell of incense in your apartment.

I don't remember where I meet you. The attraction is mutual but circumstances are against us. You've split with your girlfriend but she's not letting go, keeps an eye on you, wants you on a short leash, makes you anxious about spending time with me. One night you stay, innocently. In the morning you discover her parked outside—she's had the place staked out all night. I remember your name, what you looked like, some impressive anatomical details I discovered later.

I meet you in class. You write poetry for me. Want to go forward but your vulnerability, your honesty, scare me. I'm frightened I might damage you inadvertently and don't want the responsibility. You are in love and I'm too scared to let you in. And I still wonder if I should have dared that chance.

I meet you at an underground bar. The curiosity and attraction are mutual, perhaps mutually guarded. We see each other for months but never feel particularly close. I'm late bleeding, but it comes. I mention to you that sometimes that can happen if a woman becomes pregnant but it doesn't take. You say you're relieved and go on to say that if I was pregnant, you'd have to marry me. Yours is not a sincere proposal, or even a sincere consideration of the possible circumstance. You abandon me at the farmers' market while I buy apples. I remember your first name and vaguely what you looked like.

I meet you sometime, and somehow years later we end up together. We're comfortable, at least at first. You like to look out for me, take care of me, make me soup when

I'm sick—but demand every waking hour that I'm not working. I begin to feel crowded, cramped, claustrophobic. The relationship ends abruptly, unceremoniously. I still remember your name and what you looked like.

I meet you at an underground bar. You're a complete stranger. I take you back to my place and we try, but can't. You become frustrated with your body, frustrated with my coaxing. We lie still and touching but can't sleep. I don't remember your name or what you looked like.

I meet you when you show up on my doorstep. You're not a complete stranger, but I'd never recognized the attraction as mutual. We are crazily and instantly in love. We make love and it's the most wonderful, most perfect thing.

Then your girlfriend, the one you neglected to mention, finds out, and a letter appears in my mailbox. You insist that even though she's carrying your child, you're going to leave her. I have mixed feelings but I want to believe you. We are still crazily happy in love. Then another letter arrives, this one more threatening. Rumours start to fly around the city. I'm shunned. I'm scared. And as much as I love you, I don't see any option but to stop. It stings. I still remember your name, your body, your skin.

I go to an underground bar and drink myself stupid. On the sixth Black Russian, the bartender informs me he had to be carried home after three. The walk is cold, an event in paranoia. The stairs to my apartment are steep and dark and endless.

I meet you at an underground bar. You're not a complete stranger. Someone I've wondered about for a while. I take you back to my place. We have sex. It's not bad for a first time. Almost like making love. You hold me and I fall asleep contented, but by morning you've deserted. I develop an annoying, stinging itch, which passes quickly with the right medication. Next time I see you, you pretend we've never met.

I go to an underground bar. Looking around the room, I calculate that I've had sex with roughly a third of the patrons. At the early indications of an anxiety attack, I leave abruptly and alone.

I meet you in my building. We go out, have a few drinks too many, talk and laugh. You try to kiss me. I say, "What about your wife?" You say, "She's not here," and try to kiss me again. I give you a brief lecture on respect and walk myself home. How did I end up responsible for keeping someone else's vows?

I forget where I meet you. We hang out at the arcade, read comics, watch TV. One night inadvertently we have sex. It's familiar, friendly. A pleasant diversion. Remains a mutual physical comfort until you meet your future partner and start planning a family.

I meet you at an underground bar. You're not a complete stranger. Someone I've noticed before. I take you back to my place. We fuck. It's okay. Not great. The fumbling awkwardness of unfamiliar bodies trying to be intimate. I roll over, feel a strange push-pull. Want you maybe. Something worth exploring. In the morning you're gone but you call later. We keep company for a few weeks or months. I don't remember. I think your name was...and you looked sort of...

I meet you at an underground bar. You're not a complete stranger. Someone I've noticed. I don't remember your name or what you looked like. I take you back to my place and say, "Really, I only want a hug." We fuck anyway. Your idea and it really isn't okay. But sex is what people expect when you pick them up in bars; it's part of an unwritten contract. Want you gone.

I stop talking to people in underground bars. Focus on something that's absent. And it isn't about sex.

I meet you at an underground bar.
I meet you at an...
I meet you...

I...am sleeping alone with the radio on. The late night CBC news has a special report about a mystery killer disease causing an increase in rare cancers in the gay population of Los Angeles, although a few cases have also been reported in New York City and among Haitians and IV drug users. On first hearing, I consider how many of the men I've had sex with have had sex with other men, how many might have used drugs, how many might have travelled to and from the United States. It won't be long before this disease crosses the border into Canada, crosses the border into the heterosexual population. By rapid and inaccurate calculation, I figure I might be safe for another few months. But I decide to stop anyway. In the night, random cats come and go, checking the progress of my solitary, restless sleep.

The rock is almost skin-coloured, but unlike flesh, it's unforgiving. Smoothed by an insistent ocean, vertical cracks run into the water; age-lines, like laugh-lines, smile wrinkles gathered, collected with time. Giant rocks smoothed by the ocean's shout and beat, cracked by its weight, stained dark by its weed, pocked in places, extending into the water like a god's toes. Rocks thrown out of the water, hurled up by an enraged ocean, alive with seaweed and barnacles. Rocks tempered by the ocean's quieter moods, smoothed by its insistence, washed by its rain, graced by its birds, warmed by its sun and drowned by its sky.

The top of the rock face still resists water, each wave batter-ramming against the sheer surface, splashing up into powerless droplets. Below, the impact is greater—sounds like a door repeatedly slamming. The rock wears from below, but will it slowly cave or suddenly break and shatter down? Precarious rocks perch above me; I hear them shifting in the wind. Set back on a stone shelf, a small puddle of clear water in the sun is enough to nourish the few grasses and plants growing there like a diorama of an ancient swamp. Further on is a place where clear water drips out of rock, a steady stream from somewhere inside, somewhere beneath, cold and salty.

At the edge of the water, rock holds fossilized impressions of primeval coral: imprints of fans, fingers and brains held in hard high peaks, jagged, too rough to walk on with naked feet. Further up the beach crushed coral exchanges its identity for pink-white sand, shells leave purple-blue and white fragments like bits of broken Spode china.

The varying textures of rock: in places long flat expanses compliant with the ocean, water sliding and falling unimpeded; in places huge angular boulders resistant to waves, clifflike; in places water playing between head-sized round rocks that catch jetsam, a field of rocks smooth and round as eggs, speckled black and white. On rock flats, dents where the ocean has drilled with pebbles sometimes fill with water and stray flora or fauna, indistinguishable: the remnants of seagull meals, crab shells housing the small squirming fry of life.

This rock has iron in its soul, forms tide pools the colour of strong tea, diluted blood. Oxidization is aging; we all rust out sooner or later, even rocks. Once I round the headland, the wind is right off the ocean, clean and stiff. What's been a calm day is suddenly intense with wind, catches my breath, knocks me off balance, makes my footsteps precarious and unsure. Each headland reveals another, so I keep walking just to see what's around the next one. Imagine a fin breaking the water's surface.

The four hundred or so species of sharks are among the oldest creatures on the planet and have changed little in the last three hundred million years. All have cartilaginous skeletons, a keen sense of smell and exhibit indifference to physical injury. Some are powerful streamlined swimmers, while others are sluggish, slow moving. Some are only a few inches long while others, like the whale shark, can reach fifty feet in length and weigh thirteen tons. (Fortunately, whale sharks survive on small schooling fish and plankton.)

Many sharks segregate by size or gender for protection against larger members of their own species. Generally males stop feeding during breeding season; otherwise, the violence of the mating ritual could easily turn into a feeding frenzy. When fertile, the body of the female shark expels chemicals that permeate the water around her, attracting multiple males. The female shark has become thick-skinned; in places, her skin is four times thicker than that of her male counterpart. Lacking hands, arms, or even paws with which to position a mating partner, the male shark uses his teeth, slashing at the female and grabbing her back or fins to couple; damage is frequently sustained.

Sharks mate belly to belly with the male inserting one of his two claspers into the female's cloaca. Grooves on the clasper enable sperm to travel from the male's internal testes into the female. While all sharks reproduce through internal fertilization, a minority is oviparous, laying eggs in leathery sacs on weeds or rock. The eggs of the cookie-cutter shark hatch twelve to twenty-two months after they have been laid. Most sharks give birth to live young but the internal mechanism can be either viviparous (in which eggs mature internally with a placental connection to the mother) or ovoviviparous (in which eggs mature internally but there is no placental connection). Blue sharks, one of the best-known species, are also the most prolific breeders, having viviparous litters of twenty-five to fifty. In ovoviviparous species like the great white, fetal sharks practise oophagy—the stronger, more developed embryos dine on their less developed siblings. Pregnant females also stop feeding, their appetites returning once they are away from their young.

The cookie-cutter shark has a cigar-shaped body fourteen to twenty inches in length. Although these solitary sharks are considered a deepwater species, sinking to a depth of two miles during the day, they may rise as high as three hundred feet below the surface at night. A dark brown colour from above, cookie-cutters have bioluminescent bellies, which give an even greenish glow to their underside. Ichthyologists have speculated that this glow draws prey. The cookie-cutter uses its suction mouth to attach itself to large fish, squids and other species of sharks. It then twists its body to gouge out a plug of flesh and holds on with its tiny upper teeth while disengaging the plug with its larger triangular-shaped lower teeth; the injury is not fatal to the prey. The cookie-cutter's name is derived from the round hole it leaves when it excavates flesh. Cookie-cutters have been known to attack submarines.

Another rare mid- to deepwater shark is the aptly named goblin. This flabby, long-tailed shark is almost the colour of Caucasian skin-tone bandages—pinkish. The unlikely coloration is thought to be caused by its skin's translucence allowing the redness of its blood to show through. Unlike most sharks, it has rounded, less pronounced fins, indicating that it's a sluggish swimmer. The goblin is named for its rubbery Cyrano-esque nasal appendage, which contains electrosensory apparatus to help locate prey. The goblin has a protrusible jaw, which can extend out below its snout, giving it an appearance rather like a primitive rhinoceros. It has beady reflective eyes and sharp fanglike teeth, which it uses to capture fish and crustaceans. The species averages ten to fourteen feet in length. Because of the depth at which it dwells, no living specimen has ever been observed and little is known of its habits.

The hammerhead is one of the easiest sharks to identify, owing to the hammerlike shape of its head, with eyes located at the ends of either protuberance. Some species of hammerheads form large schools during daylight hours. Usually centred around a seamount, these schools circle calmly in the same direction. The school is generally composed of small to mid-sized individuals, in a ratio of about four females to one male. The purpose of these schools has yet to be understood, but one hypothesis is that the school offers protection to smaller sharks, and provides a meeting place for breeding partners. When hammerheads mate, they join high in the water and fall slowly, separating only when they impact on the bottom. Hammerhead schools disperse at night when individuals turn predatory. They can display exceptional acceleration and manoeuvrability, swiftly turning to attack prey with strong graceful movements. The largest subspecies, the great hammerhead, has been known to attack swimmers.

The solitary nomadic tiger shark is a bold predator. Up to eighteen feet long, the tiger is about the same length as the great white shark, but at fifteen hundred pounds it's a lighter fish. The tiger has a wide distensible jaw, broad rounded head and its upper body is camouflaged blue-green-grey with darker tiger-stripe markings. Travelling forty or fifty miles a day, at speeds sometimes exceeding twenty miles an hour, the tiger is a scavenger who surface hunts, occasionally even raising its head from the water for a better view. With serrated, curved teeth, it feeds on fish, turtles and other sharks, attacking from the surface or slightly below. Tigers have attacked and killed swimmers but have not eaten them.

Images of you caught in freeze-frame. I knew you in university and was curious-attracted. Now unexpectedly you're in the room, and there's a mutual recognition, an immediate appeal. You lean a little closer and I feel a slight change in air pressure, like a subsonic note, felt but not heard. The first touch, an embrace as we lie on the floor of my apartment locating tributaries of the Nile in an atlas. You rest your head on my breast, listen to my heartbeat. You infiltrate my unconscious. I'm inflamed by the ease with which you kiss me, touch me.

Somehow if we'd made love that first night it would've seemed contrived, forced. But now that you're not here I want you so badly I can't breathe. The need to explore a body slowly, take time to appreciate the feel, texture, taste, response; something to be savoured by degrees. The ultimate trust is actually sleeping with another—not sex. And you are still a careful thought away.

I catch myself trying to imagine you naked, the texture of your heat and skin, the perfected smoothness of boyish flesh. I ingrain your face into memory. Once captured, once scanned, I can look at you at will, manipulate the image in three dimensions—a virtual reality of the most private and primal order. In the images in my head we're intimate already.

I keep considering dialing your answering machine

long distance just to hear your voice. I'll phone back repeatedly, record the message each time, construct a loop of you to listen to as I go to sleep.

I miss you most intensely when you first leave, panic and sorrow in that initial instant of desertion. By evening I'm overwhelmed with desire. Heart in mouth, I listen to "My Boy Lollipop" in the nattering voice of Minnie Small. Feeling that moment of irrational wonder crawl up my leg, I wonder how, why, these moments occur when I'm alone and can only write them down. Try to write the epitaph to a fleeting, growing desire as it passes, unrequited.

I fall in love with you while riding a bus to Toronto, March sun flickering in and Gregory Hoskins singing "let the world call you crazy" through my headphones.

At some point sex becomes an added bonus, an addendum to the emotional. I can satisfy myself just looking at you. A touch, a kiss, and overwhelming emotion invades, pervades my body, renders the physical obsolete. The passion, the desire fulfill themselves, redefine themselves endlessly. I would be satisfied just watching you breathe.

You phone me sooner than expected. I think you do remember. There—feel it? Flinch. Sigh. Call me. I'm pulling at you. There's a trick with my mouth I'm learning to do. Remember? There's no violence in your lips, but mine bled for days. The spilt in my lower lip caused by the pressure of you trying to crawl inside me, down my throat, whole. Your skin burns my face, lips burn my flesh. That subtle pain reminds me of you.

Amazing how much time I spend with you when you're not here. Synapses turn over and there you are, vivid in voice and body. Feel you, your weight, tangible. Waking, sure I feel you inside me, and wonder what you're doing at that moment. I feel whole without you, but somehow with you I feel more three-dimensional. You voice things I've thought, but never dared say because they seemed such intimate parts of self. Somehow hearing you voice them makes me sure they're not so common, but rather extraordinary.

I want to provide you with some kind of distraction. No matter where you are I'll be there, unshakeable. A distraction of the body, mind and heart that affects you physically, visibly. A brief glance, a turn, a surrender looking for embrace.

I will only perform fellatio with you in a moving vehicle in dreams because I am a cautious person. In my half-sleep, I dream we're chatting casually in a crowded bar. I look around—everyone's watching the band. I grab your belt, hand inside your jeans, zipper open in one swift move, head down, tentatively tasting. I glance up and see the initial shock leave your face, replaced by closed eyes and that distant expression that means you've escaped. I bend down again to give you my full attention. And no one in the bar notices; they're watching the band.

You won't let yourself cum in my mouth, even though I want to swallow you. When you start to cum you lift me away, surprising me with your sudden strength. I could drown in you many times over.

You phone, say you're going to drive all night just to see me. I want you full and hard and deep. I want you inside me, all of you. You touch me and I'm flooded. Sometimes there's even a little pain, an ache. You remind me of my desire.

I look up and there you are, materialized and smiling in the sun. I try to imagine the glow of surprise on my face. There's none of the physical tension that's sometimes present after a long time. My hand touches your back so freely. I feel the fabric and your smooth heat beneath its texture. We only have a few moments to talk. After you've gone I can still see your face; it's thinner, more clearly defined. But I can't remember what you were wearing.

I see you and for the rest of the day you're everywhere. Then I recognize that my passion has little to do with you; you're only the catalyst. My passion is for a primitive construct of you, a wished-for you I accidentally burned into my visual cortex, the image projected onto a variety of human screens.

"What do you want from me?" you challenge, and I could get lost in your mouth. I want your tongue inside me. I want to play Strip Botticelli with you—no peeking and I won't deceive you with extra layers. I want your body's weight penetrating parting muscles, spreading in circles of slick dilation. I want you wet with sweat sliding over my skin.

Your rejection is as abrupt as an artery severed by a scalpel. The wound is difficult to cauterize. You accuse me of being a romantic, but you should be glad I don't have a Werther complex. I should've known things wouldn't work out when our differences in orientation became apparent: you thought the bed faced west, I thought it faced north.

Love is like trying to find my way across a frozen lake when on every previous attempt the surface has shattered and I've fallen through. You don't seem to recognize the strength that romanticism requires; there's so much pain involved.

I don't know if I can swim fast enough to be away from this moment of pain. My embarrassment at some internal inadequacy showing itself too strongly. Too contingent on your reaction, I lapse into spasms of past failure. I want to be other, want to be distant and separate but somehow still make you understand the depth and magnitude of what I'm capable of feeling, transmitted through effortless touch. But I am always not simple enough.

The darkness and depth of the depression that follows

makes me avoid professional assistance for months, unable to face what might be the final blow to a tenuous ego that such an admittance would require. Finally I acquiesce, long after the natural tide has turned. The doctor assures me I'm okay because I'm still functional, but offers me a prescription for Prozac anyway. I decline.

In the dream, I'm performing on the stage of my old high school. The auditorium is empty except for you and someone faceless you're in conversation with. I'm giving the performance of my life, craving your attention. I finish, jump from the stage to talk to you, but you walk past me with no acknowledgement, no eye contact, out a door marked EXIT.

Waking, I think, *Sorry, I thought you were someone else.*

After you blow away I still have the clarity of these images. All I'm left with is the knowledge that I'm capable of big love and that's good to know, but it doesn't seem to matter as much as I'd like it to. Sometimes I still catch flashes of you out of mind, think I've seen you on the street.

Memory has smoothed your skin. In my mind I kiss you like I mean it, a vivisection starting with your lips, a deconstruction of your heart. In time, I could amputate this love, tear every tender sinew of your body, devour every drop of blood, but still a distance from understanding. I've underestimated the complexity of desire, the weight and girth of it, the tension and anxiety held in its grinning mouth.

You were in a dream again last night; this time you were camouflaged as Johnny Depp, but I'd know you anywhere. How long is it going to take for you to stop lurking in my subconscious? I'm beginning to worry that you've found some way to hard-wire yourself in there.

I want love and so I make love happen and so I am vulnerable and restless.

The beach stretches on forever, a clear view. Sun and light shift over the water's mottled surface, ripples perpetually moving into planes of dark-light. Blue-grey-cream marbled clouds shift to the west. A seagull flies over just ahead of its fast-moving sinister twin, its shadow cast, breaking and shattered, over the cliff face. Calling into the wind, the gull flaps, but makes no forward motion.

Seaweeds gather against the shoreline, pushed there like wanton children. Stepping onto the vegetation's damp slipperiness I find it spongy, sexual, and sink into it, mired. Wonder what hidden dangers might devour me.

The barracuda is a predatory torpedo-shaped fish. Its elongated mouth features fanglike teeth, which it frequently shows, slowly opening and closing its mouth as if considering attack. A visual hunter, the barracuda is attracted to shiny objects and rapid movement. Highly manoeuvrable, it can move with amazing speed, its lithe, six-to-ten-foot silver body flashing through the water.

Living on fish of all sizes, including those of its own species, the barracuda's gape enables it to eat fish much larger than itself by bisecting them. Although generally a lone swimmer, smaller species will sometimes school, perhaps for purposes of hunting, protection or mating. Barracudas will herd schools of smaller fish into shallows and guard them like submarine shepherds until they're hungry.

The barracuda spawns in shallow protected water, although little is known of its mating ritual. Once fertilized, the eggs drift unattended. Barracuda hatchlings slowly move toward deeper and more open water as they grow.

Rarely dangerous to humans, the sight of a barracuda hanging in the water can evoke a primitive, lower brain stem sort of terror. When it does attack, often due to mistaken identity, the barracuda leaves a severe, ragged wound.

The eel is an elongated, scaleless fish with aggressive teeth. Depending on the camouflage required for its environment, coloration varies from grey-brown to bright reds and greens. The eel must continuously open and close its mouth to push water past its gills, compensating for its undersized respiratory system; consequently, even the interior of its mouth is camouflaged. The eel can also breathe through its slimy, mucous-covered skin, enabling it to survive out of water for several hours. The eel propels itself forward or backward using snakelike waves of its four-to-six-foot long muscular body. An elongated dorsal fin forms a ridge, which extends down the eel's back, merging with the caudal fin; similarly, an elongated anal fin runs the length of its belly, joining the caudal fin around the tapered tail. The eel is rarely seen during the day, preferring to lurk in rocky holes or crevices, sometimes allowing its head to protrude.

A nocturnal hunter with poor eyesight but a keen sense of smell, the eel often preys on species that are inactive during the night. Its strong jaws and sharp teeth enable it to feed on hard-shelled invertebrates such as crab, lobster, shrimp and sea urchin, as well as reef fish and octopus. When consuming larger prey, the eel uses the rotational force of its body to tear off flesh. Some species also feed on carrion.

Eels tend to spawn in warmer waters. The female lays thousands to millions of eggs, depending on the species, which are then fertilized externally by the male. In some species the egg mass is free-floating and unattended, while in others, like the wolf eel, the embryos are guarded in a nest by both parents. Hatchlings mature from an indistinguishable larval stage into juveniles and then adults. In some species, juveniles reside in freshwater until reaching maturity. Eels are thought to live thirty years or more.

Although generally considered docile, the eel can be territorial and may attack swimmers who stray too close or insert their hands or feet into its lair. Eel bites produce a bloody, ragged wound. Due to the presence of bacteria in the eel's mouth, its bites are prone to serious infection and some larger species may even be considered venomous.

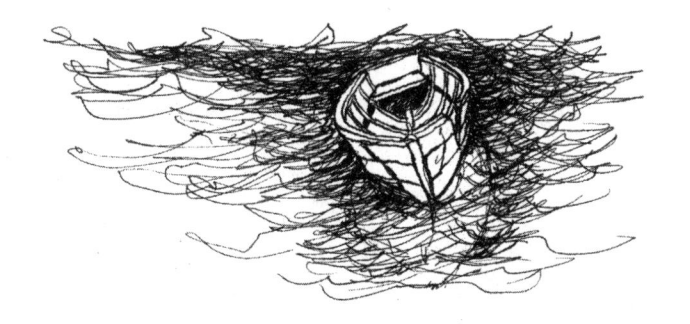

four

I find you intellectually appealing, someone to talk to in a lonely town. We have coffee, see movies, swap books. But you're insistent, persistent, want more. I push you away repeatedly, keep you at arm's length because you don't interest me beyond conversation, because you're ten years my senior and past experience makes me leery, because although you're separated you're still legally married to someone else and I don't know what that means. But you insist and in a weak, hormonally-driven moment, I finally acquiesce.

You see some kind of finality in my spur of the moment decision and there's no turning back. You say you love me; maybe I'll surprise myself, find I'm in love with you too. You want me so intensely, I rationalize, how can that be a bad thing? Wouldn't it be good to be adored? If I can't be happy in love, maybe I can make someone else happy and that's positive, right? I compromise.

I try to convince myself that you're not like my first boyfriend. After detox you went straight—don't drink, refuse drugs, even Aspirin. You are in control.

You offer me marriage and I immediately vehemently

refuse because it feels so wrong. You're still married and there's no indication of legal resolution so it's a moot offer anyway. You want me to have your old wedding ring, a simple, heavy gold band. I decline, feel uneasy, but you insist, press the ring into my hand, push it into my pocket, won't allow my refusal. I don't know what I'm supposed to do with it, so I place it in the bottom of my jewellery box and forget about it.

Because I refuse to marry you, refuse to wear your ring, you offer me a silver chain with a medallion given to you by your wife on your twenty-first birthday. Your name and the date of the event are engraved on the back. Again, I decline. This present was something between you and your wife, something given to you out of love, a fond remembrance—it's not mine to have.

Two weeks later in the park, I'm sitting on a bench with you. You get up, move behind me, say, "Close your eyes." I do, already sensing what's coming. You remove the silver chain from your neck and slip it, still warm, over my head. You put this chain around my neck, ignoring my wishes, against my will. I feel instantly shackled, incapable of escape, appendages bound.

You need a new place to live. I say, "There's a vacancy in my building," although I have doubts, am uncomfortable making the suggestion, concerned about where it might lead. Happy to avoid the work of searching for yourself, you move into the one-bedroom on the second floor with your aging dog. You maintain a separate apartment, but encroach more and more on my life.

Four days after you've moved in downstairs, I come home to find your clothes in my closet, your razor on the shelf in my bathroom. We seem to be living together, although there's been no discussion or agreement. I'm uneasy. Can't believe anyone would be so presumptuous, so invasive. Don't know what to say. Don't want to cause problems, am anxious of your reaction. I decide to give your arrangement a chance. Decide to wait a week or two and see. This is my apartment—if I ask you to leave, that will end the relationship and that might not be a bad thing.

In the throes, you promise to stay in bed with me all weekend; next morning you get up as usual, having forgotten your promise. You say, "I don't play games," and even at the time, I internally question your need to make such a statement. Until now, you've been careful to reveal only what you want me to see, practise lies of omission, encourage a skewed vision of yourself, knowing it'll be more appealing. Never trust a man whose favourite films and literature are of the *Gaslight* variety.

The third day after your invasion, my front door opens wildly, slams shut, shakes the room. You storm in like a hurricane, dark and violent, raging, throwing things, semi-coherent. One of the neighbours has said or done something. The air is electric with violence.

I stand back. Watching, distant. In seconds, barricades come up, I construct an invisible, unbreachable wall. Hold myself tight as leather, bound and gagged, I watch, eyes silent, not allowing any trace of fear to pass, keeping my face stone. You're more dangerous than anyone I've experienced—faster, stronger, less predictable. And you always carry a knife.

Now I see you. You've camouflaged yourself so well, masked your violent self successfully. I didn't know you had it in you. Insidious. The violence in you is understated but ever-present. Now it's too late to ask you to leave. I protect myself by maintaining a wall of non-communication, don't let you in. You know nothing of my heart and never will; I don't believe you ever cared to. I begin to look for escape routes, but I'm constantly anxious, vigilant of moves, statements that might inflame, might unleash more than words of anger. You confine me through your rage. Intimidation persuades the mind to work against itself, creates the *what ifs, what coulds*. Unhappy caution becomes the means of physical survival—can't address the emotional cost.

Threatened by your presence, I begin to carry a knife too, its metal clenched in my hand in my pocket. I know I'll never use it, wouldn't know how to, but handle it as a hard prop, an attempt to comfort myself—the comfort of metal on flesh.

I'm working late. You're waiting for me just inside the now locked door. A startle of breaking glass makes me look up. You casually suggest, "You'd better phone for an ambulance. Someone just bounced off the sidewalk out front." It sounds so bizarre, at first I think you're joking. But you're not.

Outside on the night sidewalk, a man lies still, unconscious and slightly bloody in a shatter of glass. The scene registers slowly. I fumble for the phone book, not sure what to do. Finally I dial the operator and ask her to send an ambulance, agree when she also suggests the police. I stare, waiting.

Emergency vehicles pull up outside, uniformed men ask questions I can't answer. Apparently a family member of one of my neighbours had taken a running jump from a second-storey window—not far enough to kill, but far enough to do some damage. The ambulance takes him, still unconscious.

I finish up. We skip the movie. Still shaky, I opt for a stiff drink instead.

On my day off, I'm home alone when an electrical outage occurs. I'm working in the breaker closet in the common hallway, attempting to resurrect power, when the man from 201 comes toward me with his friend. They're both drunk. Their bleary eyes stab me, pinning me to the wall, unflinching. They talk about me as if I'm not real, not there, a still photo in a porn magazine.

"I'd really like to fuck her. I could do it right now. Throw her down and fuck the hell out of her. Give her rug burns on her face." The friend nods and laughs ugly.

I'm trapped between the walls and the window and them. Cornered. Revert to feral. Don't show fear. Don't say anything. Close the closet with firm hands. Make myself big. Push past them sending out hard waves of electrical armour. Mount the stairs with solid heavy steps, confrontational in my retreat. Around the corner, out of their line of sight, I unlock my apartment door with shaking hands, fall inside, lock and chain the door behind me, lean against its solidity for support.

I tell you, expecting you to rage against the man in 201, expecting you to at least be a protector, hoping you will turn your rage against someone who deserves it. But you just laugh.

Despite your cool, old-hippie exterior, you're really a redneck. The difference in our politics astounds me. You're callous about the effect of events on people's lives, the human cost of violence. Your versions of history leave me speechless and there's no point in offering an opposing view; you'll only say my perspective is warped by sentimentality, tell me I'm stupid.

I'm to be home when you get there. I'm to do the domestic chores for both of us while working full-time and fulfilling your other demands. If I complain, you call me lazy. Do you think I enjoy acting the mule for groceries? Enjoy cooking food you'll complain about? Enjoy spending the hour and a half at the Auto Villa Laundromat as stray men wander in to pick through butts in the ashtrays? The couple of times you do help, it's an issue. You respond like I'm trying to turn you into a flayed sacrifice on the altar of "woman's work." It's not worth the fight.

When you have time off, you expect me to be there, but the time is usually spent watching TV. I try to convince myself that I enjoy baseball. You explain the rules of the game the way you would to a small child, paternalistic, condescending. You don't get it; I understand the rules, I just don't enjoy the game. You rhyme off statistics with pride, but I don't see the point of expending time and energy memorizing them. You quiz me on the names of baseball teams, flash their logos at me, hinge importance to me getting the right answers, when I really don't care.

Your contribution to domestic bliss is presents. You buy me things I don't need, don't want, you can't afford—then make sure I know how much they cost, make sure I understand the sacrifice you've made for my supposed happiness, make sure I understand I am to feel thankful, humbled.

An old friend visits me from out of town and you feel threatened, won't allow me to spend time with her. She asks me what's going on, why I'm so unavailable to her and I explain that her disapproval is easier to live with, less threatening, than yours. I'm not to have friends.

You know that if you manipulate me into this subservient position, I'll be too tired to say no. I lose the strength, the will, to fight back. I become your personal automaton. I start believing your persistent lies.

I want to understand what undermines me, what in me attracts abusers. I want to learn how to short-circuit the manipulation. Like a third-party observer, I watch myself reacting, hating myself all the while, feeling weak for succumbing.

I don't believe you're capable of love. What you take to be love is possessive manipulation. This isn't a relationship—it's a power struggle.

Sex with you is like lying on an assembly line folding

together sheet after sheet of the same cardboard cutout:
1. Fold in sides A(rms) and L(egs)
2. Sweat slightly to hold
3. Insert Tab P(enis) into Slot V(agina)
4. Re-insert a dozen times or so, as needed
5. Grunt once (not too loudly)
6. Remove Tab P from Slot V
7. Sleep
8. Repeat as desired, if desired, as if desired.

You wake me late in the vulnerable night with your need, your demand, and will not take no for an answer. Sex with you is an infliction, an affliction. You use your body as a weapon. My body rejects yours fundamentally, deeply, has no desire. You resort to the use of artificial lubricants. Lack of desire in the female body is much easier to ignore, to accommodate, than a similar lack in the male.

I find myself questioning the intimacy of mouth, wondering why it's easier to intermingle genitalia, retain a nonchalance, a distance from an undesirable partner simply by refusing to kiss. The mouth requires an intimacy and attention not necessary for genital sex. Hookers don't generally allow kissing; when they do, they charge extra.

A part of your routinized sex is cunnilingus. I know I should be thrilled, but your performance is raw and uncomfortable, rather than arousing. I find myself enduring your tongue, imagining all the cigarettes you've smoked, thinking of X-rated freak-show women who smoke cigarettes with their vaginas, emit perfect smoke rings into the faces of ogling onlookers. Become anxious about the possibility of developing cervical cancer translated from your mouth. I shudder, pull away repulsed. You just pull me back.

Your body inflicts unpleasurable events on mine and you block the physical hints, messages, unable or unwilling to read me. Stirring my courage, knowing comment will not be welcome, I verbalize my complaint tentatively, gently. Your response is, "I'm older than you are. I've been having sex for a lot longer than you have. I know what you like."

At some point submission just becomes easier. I give up on refusal knowing that the ensuing argument will take more time out of my sleep than acquiescence does. I'm nauseated that I too begin to use sex as a manipulation, as a weapon in this war. I fight back by making you cum so hard, so fast, you bleed. Part of me loathing this crass use of my limited power, part of me relieved at the thought of sleep in ten minutes.

And that's part of the damage, part of what I will have to unlearn: how *not* to use sex as a weapon. I try to remind myself that it's possible to make love, be intimate, possible to want sex. Possible that someday I might want my tongue on some tender part of another's body, might want another's tongue inside me.

Then we make a mistake. Or as you would have it, I make a mistake. I still don't know what happened. But there's something sacred about the first conceived— something irreplaceable.

Some magic is happening inside me where you lie still, exhausted, at rest. For once I won't let you leave. Can't you feel it too? That conjuring of cells, their growing numbers forming something exquisite and unexplainable. I'm breathless with wonder, feel sparks ricochet through my belly. Can't you feel it too?

Of course not.

I wait. I don't bleed. My body's overcome by its biology and my mind doesn't know how to react. I know what's happening, but can't admit it to myself. I pretend to deny any knowledge of what's occurring within my dark interior boundaries, beyond your control.

I'm sick, vomiting, weak. Can't keep fluids down, can't stand up without dizziness. It must be the flu. I don't bleed; sometimes illness can throw the cycle off. But the home pregnancy test tells me it's something else. I tell you and you're elated.

I don't want to be pregnant with your child, want to be someone else, somewhere else. I keep repeating, *This is not happening to me.* I want to be brave, want to do the right thing, am unsure what that is. I can't make this decision, am rendered incapable. Time is burrowing into my womb, baby steps advancing as they inevitably must if nothing is done to divert the waters of indecision. Anxiety rushes over me in a tidal wave and I'm swamped with fear.

Confused that even though I've never desired children, being pregnant causes something to shift. I'm excruciatingly aware of my body as vehicle, as vessel. I hold precious cargo that must be handled with supreme care. Protective, I drive a little more slowly, don't drink, am careful about what I swallow.

Seeking some comfort in the shower, I feel a slow heavy warmth slide down the inside of my thigh. I look, am shocked by the sudden amount of blood, the thickness of it. Hands up, I seek the stability of the hard tiles around me. A tidal pool of red existence soaks my bare feet, stains my skin. I watch it dilute and drain. Afraid of falling, I carefully slide down into the tub, sit with pink water swirling around me, slowly turning from warm to cool. Shock and relief.

I tell you when you get home. Your disappointment attacks as anger, blame.

I'm not pregnant anymore, but I'm still sick, can't keep anything down. For days, weeks, I lie on the couch in silence, feeling the weight of my body melt to dry ash, looking at the high white ceiling, watching shadows on the wall and floor as the leaves of the weeping fig move slightly from a breeze coming through the window—until dehydration forces me to close my eyes, their lids seeming to scrape shut. Overtaken by nausea I struggle to get up, try to get to the bathroom, don't make it, am sick on the living room floor, sink down in despair, hug myself to stop shaking, cry tears and sweat and can't stop, can't catch my breath. I manage to get back to the couch, lie down, try to calm myself. Watch the sunlight, will it to take me away. Close my eyes. Make myself breathe calmly, rhythmically, all the way out, expelling as much air as possible, inhaling as little as I can, willing myself not to breathe at all—a difficult thing to do. An override mechanism in the most primitive part of the brain simply won't allow it. I could die now. Everything's going to be all right...take that breath away...take that breath away...take that breath away... Will the light to gather the essential me away from this cold pain, away from this wretched body.

    I can't work for more than half a day at a time, find myself hanging off the counter, head lolling. You try to bully me into more, tell me I'm lazy, tell me I'm malingering—that shows how well you know me. Sometimes I leave just to get a break from your harassment, and as I close the door, I'm aware of you sluggishly making your way back to bed.

    You're out and I'm having a quiet evening with a little more energy than sometimes. Browsing the *TV Guide* I find a listing for a horror movie about a woman who miscarries, but still seems to be pregnant. Months later she gives birth to the son of Satan.

    An eternity of weeks shuffles by before I go to the doctor. The nausea's so bad, my weakness so complete, that after one look at me, the nurse at reception finds a place for me to lie down. Despite ten days of hemorrhaging, and despite the bleeding I've had since, the doctor thinks I may still be pregnant. He doesn't understand; this is not morning sickness—this is internal rot. This is the inability to swallow anything without vomiting, the exhaustion of waking with nausea every few minutes. This is willing the stoppage of breath. His tests are inconclusive so he sends me to the hospital.

Professional opinions conflict within the space of an hour and three floors. I'm told, "No, of course you're not still pregnant," after an overly aggressive internal examination. My veins collapsing from dehydration, I try not to pass out as they insert the IV needle. After the ultrasound, I'm told, "It looks like a perfectly normal pregnancy to me." Wheeling me though the sterile corridors, you start picking baby names.

And I already know this baby isn't going to happen. Know that even if I wanted a child, I would never want you to father any child of mine. Know this child must be damaged from the loss of blood. Know its care, your blame for its imperfections, would fall entirely on me.

The doctor has decided I'm an irresponsible girl. He believes in blackmail and will only make the necessary arrangements if I go on the pill afterwards. He ignores that the pill is contra-indicated in individuals prone to depression. I'm caught, my choices have been removed, my body has incarcerated me. I agree to do as he asks, feeling like a good little girl, while in my head I chant, *Fuck off!* as I kick him in the balls.

I have to go to Toronto for the final opinion, the assessment, the procedure. You said you'd be there. I wait, surrounded by various stages of happily pregnant women. I allow other patients to go first, look up every time the elevator doors open. Last patient of the day, I have to go in now or re-book.

I repeat the pregnancy's history, illness, spontaneous blood. The doctor's examining table borders a wall of glass that overlooks Bay Street twenty-odd floors below. This position gives me a strange, nervous sense of floating, provides the possibility of easy but drastic escape while he pushes and pokes. He questions the small-town doctors' estimate of the pregnancy's duration, thinks it's further along, into second trimester. Could entail problems of legality. Could entail a riskier, more complex, more invasive procedure. My body's aching, rigid with tension, until he decides it's easier to accept their estimate.

For the sake of formality, so I can be sure I have all the facts, so I can assure you I've tried, I ask what would happen if I decided not to intervene, if I decided to continue the pregnancy. I'm told I'd have to spend at least the next seven months in hospital; that the nausea should've passed by now and because it hasn't, it probably isn't going to; that I'd be on intravenous for the duration because of my inability to keep food and fluids down. Even then, the possibility of carrying the pregnancy to term unlikely, the chance of miscarriage high. Even then, if I managed to go full term, the chance of normal—almost nil.

I didn't want this baby in the first place and financially, psychologically, emotionally, I can't afford the price. I'm too frightened of the distance, the resentment I would feel toward anyone who would cost me so much. I say to the doctor, "If I really wanted this, could afford it, felt I was in a stable partnership with someone who'd share the responsibility, if I was close to menopause and had been trying for the last ten years and this was my only faint hope, then I'd try to hold on. But none of these is the case." The decision is obvious, but I have to wait for the availability of time and facilities. I agree to come back for the procedure after a few more weeks of nausea.

You carry no weight in this decision. I waited for you until all the other patients had gone, but you never came. I meet you in the elevator as I'm leaving and I tell you. No verbal response, just guttural. Fists against walls. I make myself small, distant in the corner, an animal looking for escape. The two of us in a metal box going down.

And so the days bring me closer to stripping away part of my soul. Leaving me more than naked. Skinning me alive from the inside. Leaving me voiceless and vulnerable.

The night before the abortion I take a long ritualistic bath. I talk to whomever's in my belly, have a vision of her as a little girl about six years old with Latino features, wearing a tattered pink gingham dress. She is about to die. I'm so sure that she will leave that life when she's still a child and come back to me. When I'm a little older, she'll be mine again. I know her genetic structure will be different, her father will be a different man. I cry salt tears into the bathwater, try to comprehend what I'm about to do, soul contorting into waves of inevitable sorrow. I hope she can forgive me. If our roles were reversed, I'm not sure I could forgive. I say goodbye quietly.

In the morning I take the bus to the hospital, nauseous and moving on autopilot. The driver yells at me to close the window, removes the last hope that the wind will blow me away.

At the hospital, in a moment of intimate death, I'm left to the mercy of strangers. Alone in the sterility of strict white and inhaled chemicals, I am slowly and deeply terrified. I'm trying to do the right thing, trying to be brave, trying to prove I can take it, trying to hold up against the torture inside my skull and heart and body.

Going under, I hear laughter from the anaesthetist and lose count. Feel my body fight the poison. Limbs thrash. Image of a fish out of water. Gasping. The bright lights of a dissection table hover over me. Bleed through my closed eyes. Try to scream but can't—it's too late. They're going to kill me. I don't want to die like this, unable to fight back. And then I'm gone.

This procedure must be painful for the child inside

me. Physically painful to be pulled away from life, sucked and scraped away into sterility, a screaming silent death.

I wake somehow. See a clock. Confused. My mind turns over slowly. Time is still here. I'm suddenly crying, relieved of the terror. A recovery room nurse is immediately beside me asking if I'm in pain. Through sobs I say, "No. I thought I was going to die." She explains that sometimes fear gets frozen, put on hold during anaesthesia, and the emotional response is the first thing to hit on recovery.

She tells me she's been instructed to keep a close eye on me, that there were problems during the procedure, more bleeding than expected. I don't want to know the details, but my mind ricochets through the possibilities: the fetus was too far along for this type of procedure and they had to remove it in pieces; I started hemorrhaging and they couldn't stop the blood; I *did* die and they brought me back.

Once shock and anaesthesia begin to wane, I'm aware of a physical relief, like the removal of a tumour, a parasite, an alien. The removal of some part of you that had physically invaded me, corrupted my flesh.

Both you and the outpatient nurse are impatient with my shaky legs. She has the good common sense to know that any unmarried girl who takes the risk of becoming pregnant deserves whatever she gets. Her stern drawn look and hard eyes require no translation.

You drive me home in silent dark, say only, "I hope you don't think I'm happy about this." I don't say anything. There's nothing to say and I'm in no shape to argue. My body's finally drawn a line in the sand. I've rejected you on the most basic cellular level. And you tried to hang on. My body can't tolerate you, can't reproduce you, can't contain or nurture you to your demands.

I wake in excruciating pain where they've ripped the

fetus from inside me. It's gone. Dead. I'm lost at a depth I thought impossible. Hollow, hollowed out, empty. I go to the living room and watch the quiet lights outside. Tears come. Deep wrenching, wailing of loss. I cry as quietly as I can, not wanting to disturb you, not wanting to wake you. Not knowing how to deal with you. Needing to be alone in my grief. You just want me to get over it, return to normal. Things between us turn even more sour—an inevitable effect of time and motion on our emotions.

I have a bath and try to talk to the child, but it's gone, too far away.

I have the need to mourn a passing that's so private, so personal. Unshared. The loss of an intimate, but one without face, without identity. There's nothing this child has touched, nothing it has left any trace of personality on—other than my womb. This child never saw sunset colours, or felt the cool sound of water on rock, or touched this love, this pain.

Tears shock the body, numb the body. I find myself not wanting body any longer. I want to be removed, elsewhere, or not at all, unspoken. Street lights glisten in the darkness through tears. And these tears are so silent—like a newborn, not born. So silent.

Abortion is a mourning of the flesh. A physical mourning with a physical sense of loss. The womb mourns what has been wrenched from it. I'm left internally scarred. Parts of the self hide behind shattered emotions, block the daylight. Dazed, I go through days automatically, knowing that if I allow myself to think, to feel, I'll lose control. You won't, can't understand, and so you create greater distance, unlock yourself from me in a cold way, make palpable degrees of separation. The intensity of my loss frightens you. I'm in a quiet alone place filled with tears, uncontrollable by three a.m.

I crucify myself wondering about where that small body has gone, now just a dead thing. Have nightmare images of black plastic bags piled in garbage heaps, small body ripped by rats. Later, I find out about hospital incineration. Body gone to ash, released to cloudy atmosphere.

I check the embryology illustrations in *Gray's Anatomy* looking for a portrait of my child. The smudgy charcoal image haunts me—human, but not quite. Then I think about what had to be done to get these sketches.

I have an urgent and immediate need to have a child. The same child that was wrenched away. Know that's impossible. It can never be the same child, cannot possibly have the same genetic makeup, will have different eyes and hair and thoughts. Confused that I never wanted children before this; that feeling now replaced by such a strong desire.

Travelling on the downtown bus, standing among strangers, feeling cold, I know that because I could kill the child within my body, I'm unfit for motherhood. I should never have children, would only damage them. I should be sterilized and be done with it. Avoid the possibility of ever becoming pregnant again.

And each of these extremes is equally strong, equally sincere, fluctuates madly from one hour to the next as my mind and heart sink their teeth in. I know I made the right decision, but the price is unexpectedly high.

The pills I'm on have just enough hormone to keep my body convinced that its reality is other than what it really is. The pills dull any remaining desire, make me feel half-dead all the time. Between the pills and the loss, I'm overwhelmed, spiralling into a devastating darkness. Every time I enter a room, I almost cry.

I want to unleash this unrest, let it run away from me. I want to breathe light again, but I don't know how to escape. I take small solace in feline company, non-judgmental. Not true—the black cat makes it plain that he doesn't like you.

Sex with you becomes even more difficult. Every time you enter me all I can think of are plastic tubes sucking out parts of broken fetus. But you decide you like the way my body looks post-abortion, broader around the hips and belly. I hate it, but it's easier to let it go, do nothing.

There's an unfortunate human tendency to cling to the familiar. To note, with regret, the time and energy already invested. Even when the familiar is damaging, it still has a hollow comfort that keeps out the cold fear of the unknown. At least I hadn't succumbed to the unplanned pregnancy method of long-term partner selection. I still had options open, even if I wasn't exercising them.

I watch your sleeping back move with waves of breath and have an urge to cut out a neat cone sample, right where your heart should be. I can see myself examining the blood on my hands by the light of the bedside lamp, looking for signs of malignancy. I imagine your blood to be black and viscous. All this I envision calmly, with the finely tuned objectivity of a medical scientist. There is no remorse.

Sleeping, I grate my teeth to wake the dead, wake from nightmares that you have removed my teeth with pliers to alleviate even that small threat. Tension mounts in my stomach, surfacing dark, overturning glimmers of communication with myself. Silent all these years, resurrecting demons in my sleep, in my haunted waking state. I fall into the deep end of memory and disappear, silenced by the demons. By morning, my mouth is stale with blood, teeth loose.

Silence hurts, is killing me like razor blades. I know it's partially of my own making and now too dense to break through. Silence hovers like a wall of sharp crystal between us. Self-censorship is a way of keeping the peace, is where bitterness begins. Turning points are easier to see once you're past them. I'm forced to deal with my emotional integrity, wonder if I'm slowly going insane.

Sometimes your attitudes startle me. The man who's been your best friend for years is gay, but you don't want to know about it. When he asks to borrow your apartment for a night to have a visit with his ex, you say, "I don't want that sort of thing going on in my apartment." I don't understand why you're so uncooperative when he asks this one favour of you, surprised at your homophobic response. I lend him my place for the night and we sleep downstairs in your place with the dog.

I walk your old dog more often than you do. He's a proud animal with his own set of regulations and I'm always a little intimidated, afraid of accidentally trespassing some unrecognized boundary. He's lonely, sits in your otherwise vacant apartment, doesn't like the city, is aging rapidly, growing ill. I can see it and question why you don't do anything for him. At my insistence you finally take him to the vet. The tumour is cancerous and too far gone.

The appointment is made, feels like an appointment with the executioner. His last night, I stay with him. You don't understand why I insist on sitting in your apartment with a bad-smelling, dying dog. He doesn't want to go to the vet's, doesn't want to stay, fights against the leash. Your last words to him are in anger, telling him to "Stay" for the last time. You leave him there alone and drive off.

You immediately need another dog. We go from the vet's to the pet store. I buy her for you, trying to assuage the pain, mine if not yours. It's a disaster. You name her after a baseball hero and try to train her but it's impossible. She needs more time and exercise than you're willing to give. I try, but I don't know dogs and have limited time myself.

Your behaviour around animals assures me again of my decision not to have your child. I can see the damage you would do.

When I try to exert my small will, do something I want to, you become ill—another manipulation designed to provoke guilt. I arrange a holiday weekend in Toronto alone and you develop an excruciating headache. I offer to stay, not wanting to, and you look at me through watery eyes and whisper, "No, it's okay," hoping I'll insist. I don't. Instead I leave, refusing to let you slow me down.

I haven't been alone, haven't been to Toronto for fun, in years. I revel in my freedom, almost squirming in it like a puppy. The train journey is relatively short, vibration of motion transmitting up my body, sun coming in like strobe light as we pass stands of bare trees. The hotel room is clean and spacious and the TV gets stations I can't get at home. I raid the room fridge for gin and tonic and junk food, order room service, spend my evenings soaking in bubbles in the huge tub in the dimly lit bathroom, spend my days wandering up and down Yonge Street. The sun is starting to strengthen with spring light and it's brilliant cold. The street has a live electricity, enticing, invigorating, joyous. I don't want to leave.

When I return, you inform me you've spent a horrible weekend in bed in agony. I won't be forgiven.

That taste of freedom renews my search for escape. I've heard people say, "You shouldn't stay in an abusive relationship. Just leave." They've clearly never been in one. It isn't that simple. Intimidation is strong medicine. You're strong, quick-tempered, always armed. My mind works hard against me in an effort to avoid physical injury, somehow discounting the emotional and psychological toll. I exercise an unhappy caution as a means of survival. I know what move to make—what I need to figure out is how and when to make my move without sustaining injury. I will not be a victim. I consider buying a gun.

In an effort to re-exert some control over my life, I go back to school. You resent the time I spend with other people. After class, several of us go for a drink. I have a gin and tonic and get home about eleven-thirty. You aren't working that night and have been sitting alone with the TV set, waiting for me.

"What kind of time is this to get in?" you demand like a petulant father. I'm shocked, outraged that you think you have the right to dictate every second of my life.

Finally, the slow methodical shuffle of your divorce papers concludes. I'm anxious that with the legal coast clear, you'll again insist we marry. I won't. As with all extreme changes, there are intensely mixed, confused emotions. Your divorce from her somehow feels like a divorce from me. When I tell you this, you don't understand, but I can't explain it any other way. Something to do with the disjunctures in our relationship, the ways in which we have never been a couple and never will be.

You make a point of telling me you've never slept with a woman over thirty. I'm dangerously close to that now. Individuals too intent on fighting the inevitability of aging are probably not a good bet for long-term commitment.

I'm at the laundromat folding your damn socks into a neat pile. It's always here that I get angry, resentful, think about getting out. The folding of laundry is therapeutic, the heat of the fabric a comfort. Always by the time the clothes are folded and bagged, I've calmed. But not today. Today I know that continuing to tolerate this relationship is stupid and unnecessary. When I go home, I'm going to tell you it's over. And although I recognize the potential for violence, I'm angry enough that I'm past being afraid of your reaction, beyond intimidation. I smile, feel strong. The sun comes out as I walk home.

Then you surprise me, beat me to the punch. You say

you're moving out; I readily agree. It's better this way—no violence. Better for you to think you're making the decision. I thought you'd never let go.

Sleep. I knew I was tired but hadn't realized how sleep deprived you'd kept me. The luxury of enough, revelling in the freedom of my uncompromised bed. Memory of calm infiltrates, a memory crawling and pulling like an infant. Too much memory, too full already, past overweighing future, and like a diver, perched too close to the edge, I fall into the deep end of memory and disappear. Silent demons in my sleep; I don't remember my dreams.

I'd hoped to be entirely free of you, but you won't let go, expect to see me for before-work coffee, after-work coffee, conversation into the evening—occasional sex. It's difficult to break a physical habit of years. I still don't have my life back, only my bed. I ask you to move the rest of your things out of my apartment and you respond, "What's the rush? You're not seeing anyone."

I ask you about the woman you're working with. Searching for an excuse to back away further, I say, "If you two are at the beginning of a relationship, that's fine. But *we* shouldn't be spending as much time together as we are, shouldn't be having sex at all. It's not fair to anyone."

And you reply, "No. It's nothing like that."

Our before-work coffee conversation is designed so that a moment before you know I have to leave, you drop a bombshell. You and she will go to Australia together. I have a moment of shock, then I have to leave, spend the morning at work feigning pleasantries. Hold on until lunch to get things straight. Paranoid, I begin to feel that everything you say is targeted.

I know that the only person who can pull away, establish new ground rules, is me. I tell you I won't be joining you for morning coffee anymore. Small, easy steps. Still feeling too threatened, too weak to do anything more, I back away from you cautiously, make no sudden moves.

I see her at a show. We chat amicably enough. The small child of a friend distracts her. She says, "Just one more big adventure and then I'd like to have one of these."

You've already told me that you and she are not intimate and I choose to believe you. After the years I've known you, I know you wouldn't lie to me. But my gut doesn't agree. I ask you again about your relationship with her and again you deny anything's going on. Again, I choose to believe you, doubt gnawing inside me.

She and I are talking in the bar you're working at. We've both suspected. We calculate the overlap of time between our two situations—you've lied to us both. Like a high school gossip she furthers the conversation into the matter of your sexual prowess. I tell her I find you disappointing, boring, surprised at my own cold candour. I've never spoken to anyone about anyone this way. She says she thinks you're a wonderful lover and I find myself wondering who she's slept with. Now that the truth is out, she has words with you, leaves in anger.

I sit very quietly. Inside I'm nodding, thinking, *I knew it*. I feel very calm. Somehow this clarification frees me entirely from your expectations.

You were running stupid and unnecessary risks, creating tensions between yourself and people you purportedly cared about. I tried to make things easier on everyone concerned, tried to give you an easy out. All you had to do was say yes when I asked about your relationship with her. How could I have made it any simpler, cleaner?

We walk in the park in the sun. You say that both she and I have questioned the involvement of the *other* woman. You've lied to us both consistently. When I ask you why, you say, "It's none of your business who I sleep with." And maybe now you're right, but when we were living together, when you and I were still having sex? You defend your right to lie to the woman you've just started seeing. You have a curious sense of respect, no notion of the impact of your actions on others.

I seek advice on AIDS. Take it under advisement.

I work, go home, avoid going out, avoid people. This is a small town and everyone else knew about your affair, watched me floundering. I feel I can trust no one, don't want to hear the whispers, don't want to answer the questions.

You tell me you need me around for intelligent conversation, but I have no need to talk to you. She leaves town and you want me close by. I refuse. You think I'm a bitch for distancing myself, taking my life back, shrugging off your excess weight. I'm tired of feeling middle-aged before thirty. For the first time in your adult life you're truly alone. It's time you learned to fly solo.

Christmastime, I've got an extra day off work. You call me up to see if I want to do brunch, sort of a *let bygones be* deal—it's Christmas after all. We're seated in the smoking section at your request. We order, but the restaurant's busy. While we wait, we talk.

You say, "You know, things between her and I are serious."

And I say, "I know."

"No, I mean, *really* serious."

"Yes, I know that."

"We've been keeping in touch, writing letters while she's been away. When she gets back, we're going to get married."

Why are you telling me this? You've already made it clear that your relationship with her is none of my business. Am I supposed to be happy for you? Given the ways you've hurt me, that's expecting too much. I feel like you're rubbing my nose in my inability to give you what you wanted, showing me that you can get it elsewhere.

I pick up the glass of ice water by my left hand. I watch as my fingers curl around its hard, slippery, condensation-covered surface. I consider, for a moment, pouring it over your head, but I'm not big on public scenes. I take a meditative sip. I look to my left and see the exit, consider getting up and walking away, just leaving you sitting here alone with a puzzled look on your face. For some reason I don't do that either.

For this long moment, I'm fighting for control. Take another sip of water. Breathe. Raise my eyes to you and say, "You're nuts, you know that? Absolutely nuts."

When I tell you, "You two are going to kill each other," you say, "I know. That's what I like about it." Don't say I didn't warn you. And don't expect me to be there to pick up the pieces.

Then she's back in town. You and she are doing a gig together in Toronto and will be gone for a few days, back late. You ask me to walk the dog. I'm uneasy, want to say no, but don't. I convince myself that I'm walking the dog for the sake of the dog, not as a favour to you.

Just after one in the morning, the phone rings. The security company informs me that the alarm at work has gone off. It's just past bar-closing time, might be the real thing. I go down to find the police already inside, having made their way through the broken glass door. Shards and pebbles of glass are scattered over the floor, a bin's knocked over, there's blood. Two passersby caught the guy in the back alley struggling with a duffle bag full of stolen property. I call the owner, the insurance company, the glass company. By about three a.m. I'm upstairs in bed listening as the remaining glass is smashed out of the door frame to make way for the new whole pane.

In the morning, the recovered merchandise is displayed neatly on the floor where the police have photographed it for evidence. The worst of the glass is gone, but we'll be vacuuming up slivers for weeks. I spend the morning cleaning up blood with antiseptic soap. I wear gloves, am anxious.

After a sleepless night, and at the end of this difficult day, I enter your apartment to walk the dog. The pup leads me directly to the back bedroom where you and she have laid out your new makeshift double bed on the floor. I feel I'm invading privacy, feel like you've planned this. Aloud, I say, "I don't need this shit." I go upstairs.

Your razor's still in my bathroom cabinet. Books and papers and other pieces of your existence are still scattered about my apartment. I've asked you three times now to please remove them. You haven't, although it's been months since you lived here. I pack your things into a box, still having to play your maid, do this one last thing for you if I want it done.

I write a long, pointed letter saying everything I needed to say to you at that moment. All I remember of it is, "You are the most selfish, disrespectful individual I have ever known." And I asked for my keys back.

I walk the dog for the last time, say goodbye to her and she seems unusually subdued. I leave the box of your belongings, the letter, the wedding ring you gave me to hold so you could breathe without the weight of its failure. I never wanted it; now I return it to you, cold and unworn. I'm not carrying your baggage any further. I lock up and push the keys to your apartment under the door. Your little monkey's slipped her leash.

The term *emotional abuse* kept ringing in my head, and I thought I was being paranoid, melodramatic—until other people verbalized it, suggested it was appropriate. Your machinations seemed like malicious behaviour, and I thought I was overreacting—until your ex told me I was right.

You're still too close. Bitterness does not cleanse easily; it re-emerges at the slightest provocation, merest afterthought. Tremors of past lives erupt, sending sparks into ignition. Casual comments cast aside unmeaningly, innocently, astound me into internal ricochets. My defences are too easily deployed. Shrapnel, unable to pierce the armour I've forged, bangs around inside, ripping me to shreds. I'm afraid that when the flak jacket's removed, there may be nothing left but damage.

I feel too much and too little simultaneously. Numbed, I find a need for physical pain to reunite body with soul. I get three holes punched in my left earlobe on the same day. The pain is strangely refreshing, like pouring ice water on the soul. A way of re-establishing control over my body, taking control away from you.

The long tense silence between us pervades the whole building. I'm gaining strength all the time. After a month, I have more things I need to say to you, have clarified my thoughts into a rich, digitally pure challenge, have accepted the possibility that you might become violent. My need to speak is now stronger than my fear of physical injury. I'm willing to take a beating if that's what's required to be heard.

I call you up for coffee, say, "There are still things we need to talk about." You agree, walk upstairs allowing me home turf advantage. You've never seen me like this, didn't know I was capable, have underestimated your opponent. Submission doesn't suit me and you've far surpassed my limited tolerance for it. I'm furious, but dangerously controlled. I deliver careful words with quiet intensity, my mind functioning like a cleanly oiled steel trap.

You become flustered, and when you slip on your words, I catch you. Now you have to admit that while we were still living together, you had sex with numerous partners, not just her. I was one of many, despite our supposed commitment. I know your aversion to condoms, am anxious, know I need to have an AIDS test.

Throughout the conversation I feel empowered, in control. And something unexpected happens, something I hadn't foreseen. The intimidation I'd let control me for so many years isn't just gone—it reverses. You hadn't realized I was this capable of standing up to you, challenging you, catching you up on your own lies—and I was too intimidated to try. Now that I've braved you, overcome my fear, you have nothing left to challenge me with.

And I experience a further trickle-down effect: the last remaining piece of the structure that is me, is mortared back into place. Whole again at last, I rediscover the strength and daring I had in my teens. But now I'm also armed with the knowledge of experience, have tested the fortifications, know where the boundaries are, when I have to retreat—and that makes me feel truly indestructible. A not-so-naïve innocence emerges.

The price of intimate companionship always seems too high. I need to be selfish for a while and I'm not going to apologize for it. I need to explore myself, establish my own path. I retreat into my music. There will be no more yous.

You tried to sweep me off my feet, but it was about throwing me off balance and gaining control. Self-perpetuated feelings of guilt and weakness accompany the abuse so the target of the manipulation is never quite sure whom to blame—not an easy vortex to escape. Of course, I know you don't see yourself as abusive—abusers never do. Just like the recipients of abuse don't always see themselves as abused, manipulated, until they get far enough away, until they get third-party input.

I used to believe the line between insensitivity and abusiveness lay in maliciousness, but now I'm not so sure. Maybe it lies at self-centered egotism, the sheer inability to perceive the needs or desires of another.

I'm asked, "Why did you put up with it?" I *was* aware of the abuse, at least to a degree. Part of me simply wanted to understand it, try to find ways of short-circuiting it. But I never succeeded. And somehow it had something to do with proving I was tough enough, could take it. Proving that to...myself? Why? Maybe that's where it ends—when I can't answer my own questions. But there's no clear motivation. Rather, a lack of motivation, a lack of direction. A lack of caring about myself.

Sometimes life seems like little more than damage control. I have to question why I make the same mistakes repeatedly. Significant others always seem to lose their significance. I have to bring myself to the painful realization that some people just aren't worth the effort. It hurts me to admit that, but it's the only way I can protect myself.

The ocean tucks its feet in for low tide, regroups and then attacks again, a slow turnaround, rocking back and forth, balancing between distant shores. Traces of ocean are left in tide pools, sparks of life dancing, barely detected. In one, rust-coloured rock contrasts with hundreds of small blue bivalves. Fry move so that at first they seem imagined, ripples of shadow-light wriggling. When the turnaround comes, the rocks are almost drowned, overwhelmed, sudden islands appear and disappear. I could drown just by staying in the same place for too long.

Heavy thunder rolls in the tropical distance. I see storm illuminating sky and water, see the disruption on the surface as drops embed themselves, become one with the body of the ocean. Below the surface, it's dark calm.

Generally a sluggish fish, the stonefish spends most of its time resting on the bottom of rocky areas or coral reefs, or sometimes buries itself in the sand using its large pectoral fins. The stonefish is the world's most venomous fish, although it's fairly small, generally twelve to fifteen inches in length. It uses perfect commando camouflage: its skin is grey-brown, has irregular warty bits and fleshy protrusions, and is sometimes even covered with algae. The stonefish has a large upturned head with a wide gaping mouth and glaring red beady eyes.

Stonefish feed on other fish and crustaceans. When prey swims past, the stonefish moves with such rapidity that its feeding behaviour can only be captured by high-speed camera equipment. The sudden opening of its wide mouth causes the prey to be sucked in.

If a stonefish feels threatened, it erects the thirteen spines along its dorsal fin. Should the intruder exert downward pressure on the spines, these needlelike appendages will puncture the skin, penetrating shoes, fins, or the heavy leather of a ray or shark—the stonefish's main predators. Acting like the detonator of a landmine, downward pressure on the spine triggers the injection of white viscous poison. This poison, of unknown chemistry, is produced by glands at the base of the spines and travels along grooves into the victim. The poison produces excruciating pain, intense burning, throbbing, swelling, fever, muscle twitches and respiratory depression. A whitening of the skin around the site of the sting occurs as the oxygen supply to the area decreases. Severe cases can also cause vomiting, delirium, shock and tissue damage necessitating amputation. A sting from a stonefish can be fatal. Swimmers who have recovered have reported suffering from pain and after-effects for months.

The mating behaviour of the stonefish has not been documented, however, that of the lionfish—a more flamboyant, less poisonous relative—is on record. Fewer male lionfish occur in the population, and during mating, a single male will group with four or five females. At dusk, the male seeks out a female and rests beside her, looking starward, before initiating a courting dance by ascending and descending in the water. The female joins him until both fish meet near the water's surface. In some subspecies the male may nibble at the skin flaps on the female's chin, an activity which seems to cause arousal. The female releases two egg tubes into the water, which the male then fertilizes. Given the poisonous nature of these species, internal fertilization would be a nasty proposition.

The giant clam resides on the bottom of shallows or coral reefs. This largest of bivalves may weigh over five hundred pounds and measure over four feet in length. The clam feeds on micro-organisms filtered from the surrounding water, and also has a symbiotic relationship with zoxanthelle, a specific type of photosynthetic algae. By living on the clam's upward-facing mantle, the zoxanthelle are positioned for the optimal light absorption they require; in return, they create sugars and amino acids, which are directly ingested by their host.

The giant clam is a hermaphrodite; initially it matures as a male, but later it develops gonads capable of releasing both sperm and eggs. When ready to spawn, the viscera surrounding the gonad turns from a dull brown colour to bright orange. When individuals reach sexual maturity, their sperm are released prior to the release of the eggs, perhaps to reduce the incidence of self-fertilization.

The shell of the giant clam is oriented so its hinge rests on the bottom with the opening pointing upward, toward the water's surface. The shell's exterior is usually rough with toothed or fluted edges. Extruding beyond the shell is the mantle, which resembles full pouting labial lips, and is coloured brown-green with green or blue patches. Although often open for feeding, the shell will slowly close if the clam feels threatened.

five

Safe is a lethargic state of mind. The only real *safe* physically or emotionally is auto-eroticism: no birth control needed, no broken hearts, satisfaction guaranteed. Since your stumbled admission of multiple partners, Eros and Thanatos have been dancing a jig in my head. My mind keeps spinning through *what if* scenarios. What had you been doing? Who with? I don't want to be a statistic, face the possibility of a premature painful death, am numb, have trouble sleeping.

At night I walk in search of answers; the possibilities terrify me. I find myself in the red-light district, men slow their cars to look, proposition me. Unplanned, I'm at the doors of the Sexual Health Clinic. I didn't know I knew the address. The street entrance is open, but the interior office doors are locked. The adjoining needle exchange office shines its light into the hallway and people shuffle in and out. When the couple working there sees me, they offer free condoms. I reply that I don't need them because I'm never having sex again. They look dubious and hand me pamphlets instead. Turning to leave, I'm faced with a man who looks about fifty, might only be thirty, eyes me suspiciously. I go home to a cold, clean bed.

I try to dial the number of the clinic, hang up, breathe deeply, dial again. I ask questions like an anonymous bystander whose life could never be affected by HIV. My initial nervousness gives way. Fright causes me to follow through, make the appointment.

The counsellor asks, "How do you think you'd react if the results were positive?"

I look at the floor, my shoes, shadows filigreed on the carpet. It isn't a question I'm ready for, haven't thought it through that far. I look past him, out the window and reply, "I think I'd go down to the river and sit and cry for a while. Then I'd probably go home and figure out my priorities, determine what I still need to accomplish."

He looks at me and I can't avoid his eyes. "That's the first time anyone's *admitted* to me they'd have an emotional reaction."

I'm relieved to talk to someone. I tell the counsellor the whole story, tell him I think I'm being paranoid. He doesn't pass comment either way, but points out that having the test would at least remove the stress of not knowing. Then he asks how I feel, not just about the test, but about the situation. My stomach claws its way up my throat and lodges there. I look at the door, willing myself to be on the other side of it. All I can think is, *This isn't happening to me; it's a bad movie and I want to find the exit.* I know he's watching me, still expecting an answer. I swallow back the threat of lost control and admit to a twisted combination of crying fear and absolute rage.

A nurse takes some of my blood, collects it in a series of vials. I watch blood exit my arm, going away from me. Mine, not mine. The objectification of blood for purposes of testing. Something inside tightens, almost gags, but I maintain the outward façade of a disinterested onlooker. The name on the vials isn't mine—it's a construct. Not quite anonymous, but pseudonymous, yet the results of the tests on this blood will relate back to my body.

I walk on gilded splinters, balance on the wire between a *yes* or a *no* that changes a life. There will be two weeks of waiting. I go home and promise myself I won't think about the test results, will be calm.

I have to try to view the situation with the mathematical precision of Bach, concentrate on the interweaving of contrapuntal lines and see where they take me. But Gould plays with a touch that makes the notes fly until the rationality of the score fractures, I find myself unable to follow the clear path of each line as I encounter the dense growth of other lines. Precision becomes another tool for the heart, for a passion not expended on lovers. Emotions swirl like Bach's counterpoint. I don't know where the thematic statement begins or ends—the record's too warped and the needle skips repeatedly in its grooves. I'm like a contrapuntal theme in flux, in a constant state of chaos churning in my own wreckage. I don't know what to do, so I try to ride the waves and pray like I know how to. I keep wanting to wake up, but sometimes I feel nearer to death than waking.

My body feels like a time bomb looking for someplace to go off and I don't want to be around when it does. My body feels like a tomb already. If I'm ill, I'll be treated as a diseased person, like a leper. Some things don't change much, especially the human reaction of fear to the unknown, the unresolved, the disease with no cure. I'll be treated as the body in bed number seventeen, be pricked and handled like a piece of raw meat, only be touched with rubber gloves. No human contact, no skin, no warmth. I will want to bite them just to prove the point that I'm animal, not vegetable.

I can't sleep, close in on myself, go walking. I'm struck by the size and surreality of all things, the speed of their motion. Light reflects differently now; it glistens, has more depth. The air that fills my lungs is cold and sometimes hurts.

I'm dirty and diseased on the inside and no amount of water can cleanse that. I listen to Marianne Faithfull retching the words to "Why'd Ya Do It?" Play it loudly and repeatedly, get vengeful ideas I know I'll never act on.

Does anyone remember what my favourite colour is? This is important. It's blue. At least it's been blue for a long time—it wasn't always. And that's only one detail. I remember the garden in the house I lived in when I was young, my first day of school, riding on the back of a horse too far off the ground, clouds from summer skies and the smell of autumn air. And I remember all this as no one else can, as part of my existence. All this will be lost. There's no way to record it, to hold onto it. Where does memory go? Lost. But I'm no good at letting go, never have been.

I look around the apartment at things I've collected. Items I've found, have bought, been given—find them of no significance or comfort, their weight cumbersome and meaningless. For a moment I want to free myself from the bonds of these material objects, envision myself hurling them out the window, but it isn't worth the effort.

I put on Mozart's Requiem, lie on the living room floor, close my eyes, listen, turn up the volume and feel a smile form on my lips, float. By the time the angelic sopranos enter during the Confutatis, I'm in heaven. Death music written on a deathbed. Mozart must have already been hearing the sounds of heaven.

I get a book out of the library when I'm feeling particularly serious, morose. I read about the common stages of those facing death: denial, anger, bargaining, depression and finally acceptance. It seems an oversimplification, an attempt at clear-cutting the emotional tension, making death quantifiable, manageable from an objective distance. Morbid fear and rage are not understandable in any rational way, can't be isolated to words typed on a page.

Picking my way through the day, through the night, I try to dissect the confusion of emotions that fall on me. Everything means too much and not enough all at the same time. I'm too sensitive to light, to thought, to touch. Careful—I might combust, I might float away or drown at any moment. I am drowning, but no one's noticed. I watch myself closely, sure to keep the mask in place at all times. Either I'm a better actor than I knew, or no one really wants to know.

In the mirror, my face, my body, have changed. The face is serious, crazed, the eyes dark. I've lost weight. The bones of my pelvis and ribs protrude. I see my body as object with the same physical materiality as the things in the room. Even in the mirror I can stand apart from it, view it with disdain as a diseased tissue. I don't want this pointless weight, am always struggling against the touch of gravity. I am become a pair of eyes. If the hand of death touches me, then no other hand can threaten me. There's no fear that I can fall prey to now, except that of death itself.

In my head Mary Margaret O'Hara contorts through "Body's in Trouble." The push-pull rhythm of that, the need to go forward, reach out, be held, be comforted.

I could handle death better than this uncertainty. Not knowing is driving me away from the rest of humanity, driving me to cravings for non-existence. It's not the death itself that frightens me; it's the possibility of decrepitude. I don't want to suffer, don't want to lose bodily functions while my mind is still active. And I don't want to lose my mind.

Time becomes totally relevant and irrelevant all at once. I begin to see how young I am. I've wasted so much time and life and energy, haven't had a chance to do anything yet and there's so much to do. The time on the clock offers no meaning, I've stopped wearing a watch, do things at the time that feels correct. Real time, lived time, becomes frightening and precious, can't be wasted. I have things to do, so many I can't name them all, but I don't know where to start.

It's getting cold at night. I put on an old overcoat that used to be my Dad's. It's too big and envelops me like a hug. I hide inside it, wishing for invisibility, wishing to be taken back to the thought before all this, wishing not to be. No one knows but me, and alone I struggle to take the weight. Heaviness surrounds me like a shroud borne too soon. I want to cast it off, be light, float into the night sky unfettered. I thought there'd be someone here, a warmth on the skin of my hand, a shared breath. Someone to talk to who would know what to say, when to be silent. I shrug myself deeper into the coat, feel like a shadow.

Górecki's memorial for the long dead, the *Symphony of Sorrowful Songs*, grows in deep organic waves, breaths of sound. The double basses creep into the first Lento like dusk settling on the quiet, like dust settling on bone, and then that restless Aeolian mode rises to the single notes of heaven in the soprano prayer of the "Holy Cross Lament." The power of that elevation, that elation. Then it descends back to earth and crawls into the dark again.

I contemplate the horrors of what might be happening within my skin. I've started to smoke, and pacing the floor like a ravaged tiger, I consider options, consider how to proceed if... Someone tells me he once held the hand of a woman while her fingers were amputated; as a result of AIDS, gangrene had blackened them. I can't get that image out of my mind. My fingers curl instinctively, cup themselves close to my palms.

How long can I go without touching another human

being? It's starting to hurt, create a vacuum inside me. Sometimes I find it hard to breathe.

It's cold outside. I've lost more weight and although I'm feeling okay, the cold sinks into me too quickly. I can't get warm. It's too much like the hand of death reaching inside my body to stop my heart prematurely. I have a hard enough time fighting the cold that's permanently lodged in my stomach, the cold that prevents me from eating.

I don't think I wanted this existence in the first place, don't recall being asked. It would be so much less painful, so much gentler on the soul, not to be. The terror of transfiguration, disfiguration of flesh decomposing while I'm still inside. Bitterness sets in like the taste of rotting fruit. I don't want to be like this.

I become death obsessive, start experimenting. Every time I cross the road I imagine a truck taking me, clean and painless. Would it be okay at this moment? At this moment...at this moment...would it be okay? The first few times there are tears in my eyes, tears of loss, the mourning of my own mortality. Then, just before I raise my right foot to take the curb on the other side, it *is* okay. I could die now.

I start collecting memento mori. Dead roses pulled from someone else's garbage, the ashes of incense sticks, the chain from the neck of a long-deceased dog, fingernail clippings, costume jewellery from estate sales, creased sepia photographs of people I've never met—then the angels. Postcards, etchings, cardboard cut-outs of angels, statuettes, gold brooches, carved reliefs of angels. I make a shrine of angels and dead flowers in the living room, surround it with the other mementos and light candles. Having no predetermined rituals to ascribe to, I make up my own as I go along.

I'm contemplating cremation. I'm repulsed by the idea

of rot, afraid that if I'm ill, I will have had enough of rot by the time my body lets me go. I like the idea of a purge by fire, consumption by flame, ascending with the heat and smoke, defying gravity at last, an elevating consummation. And then maybe I'll have the ashes dropped from a great height through the air into water, completing the elemental circle.

My guardian angels seem to have left me at some point. Maybe I stopped believing in them, so they went away. Maybe I can persuade them to come back; I need them now. Sometimes I can see them, a flicker at the corner of my eye. As I turn my head, I know it's already gone. Who will lead me to the clouds? I'm afraid of losing my way.

Maybe I'm going to die soon, but what was I expecting? I'm taking this all far too seriously. I want to ascend into the heavens laughing, but I'm not sure I can laugh that hard any more.

I've started thinking about my funeral—not plotting it on paper, just fantasizing. I know it won't be remotely like the fantasy, but having led an insignificant life to date, I'd prefer to pretend that I might have a significant funeral. One likes to believe that the loss of one's face from the landscape will be noticed. I envision a swarm of faceless mourners in uniform black peering through a grey mist. I want the horse-drawn hearse from the museum to carry me, the one with the brass ornamentation and the highly polished carved wooden vines. Its team of blinkered heavy horses with black-dyed plumed headdresses clumps by solemnly. The mourners have one last sorrowful look at the casket, weighted with perfumed flowers of all shapes and colours.

I haven't picked the music yet—there's so much to choose from. I want something solemn for the procession; maybe the weight of Michael Nyman's "Memorial," and then something verging on a demonic *danse macabre* to swell up out of the ground at the burial site. Imagine the fourth movement of Berlioz's *Symphonie fantastique* regurgitated by the earth, the tympani causing slight tremors, the horses terrified into a gallop by the brass and all hell breaking loose as the carriage topples into the "Witches' Sabbath" of the final movement. Past the bells tolling the rhythm of the dead, I will rise up with the Dies Irae and join the witches in my former lover's torment. Highly melodramatic, but very satisfying.

I think about hiring a hit man. The contract would stipulate that as soon as I started to show signs of failing, he'd do the job. The method would have to be unexpected, painless, quick, but I'd also like something sort of stirring and theatrical, maybe something that would make the news. If I hired a hit man, it would lighten the weight of this problem, would make it somebody else's responsibility. But that's why we hire professionals, right?

I go walking again. I always look before crossing; I was well taught. I know there's no car coming. It appears by chance occurrence, a quantum blip of an apparition, the loud horn breaking my distraction. I leap back, feel the brush of wind and road dust pass and sting my cheek. Maybe I'm becoming suicidal in a passive way, this act of violence sneaking up on me gently, subconsciously. I'll be dead before I know I've wished it, before I realize I've made it happen.

I stop even trying to sleep at night. I walk, restless, putting pieces together, watching bats and nighthawks; there's no sound other than their screaming. Some nights there's anger, other nights tears. I pass a blood donor clinic. I used to give blood regularly, used to have the organ donor card on my driver's licence filled out—an attempt at immortality, or prolongation anyway. There was power in the thought that some part of the body I'd taken for granted could survive my personal demise.

I find myself in a bar, decide to have a drink. I study people, watch as a couple gets up to leave together and something inside me strains. I stop myself from jumping in front of them and delivering a stern lecture on safer sex and STDs, stop myself from thrusting condoms into their hands. I get drunk. A stupid thing to do, a vain attempt at feeling better, a grasping at straws, a quick fix, a failed attempt at escape. I end up sick and sweating with the shakes. Depression and morbidity eventually become rage—at you, at the situation, at myself. I collapse in tears of frustration and fear.

The only people out this late are the street cleaners, the after-hours drunks, and me. I sit on a bench at the edge of the park and watch a man repainting the lines of the parking spaces. The *shush* of the spray machine cuts through the city's low hum with a regular rhythm. The lines delineate the space provided for each car, but when I try to imagine my body as a car, the lines become hazy, in need of redefinition. I need a place to park but can't find a clearly delineated space, so I keep going, travelling in circles around the same dark block.

I need somebody to be here, but what I need can't be discussed over a single drink, or even two or three. What I need can't be accomplished in a night of belly-to-belly sweating. Besides, I don't remember the last time I had sex I really enjoyed. I admit that there are still moments of craving that act of consummation, for tongues to melt together, but the desire's immediately cut short by the thought that it's unsafe—emotionally and physically. Sex is just a more pleasurable kind of death wish, a way of ensuring slow suicide while avoiding personal responsibility.

As an experiment, I try one of the sex phone lines. It's free and anonymous, like an AIDS test, for the first five minutes. I listen, feeling like an eavesdropper. The talk is sexual in the most banal manner, doesn't have the eloquence of a Nicholson Baker novel. I lose interest and hang up before my free time runs out. All those passionate late-night movie kisses...how much safer life would be in Bogart's arms.

There's no one who would drive all night if I needed them. What I need—the closeness, the love, the trust I need—takes time to develop, and I'm not sure I have enough time. I'm afraid of being too utterly alone at death. Maybe I'll surprise myself. Maybe I'm stronger than I feel right now.

I need to turn the tension in my soul into fire, need to find a way to cleanse myself of bitterness. The amount of negative energy I've allowed myself to generate, have revelled in, is frightening. I must find a way to dissipate it before it consumes me. I play Michael Nyman's "Miserere" repeatedly, letting the purity of the boy soprano sink deeply into me.

I don't want to be bitter anymore—it takes too much effort, too much energy and it scalds the soul. I've become manic about trying to accomplish all the things I've always thought about doing but haven't done yet. I need to do everything now, all at once, while I can still grasp the time. I need that immediacy, crave new experiences.

I need a change of atmosphere, need to get off the ground. I climb the fire escape to the roof of one of the old red-brick five-storeys downtown. Up here it's colder, windier, more alive. I want to fly, be helium-filled, lighter than air, lighter than sky. I look down and feel my stomach threaten to leave my body. I step back. The gap between this building and the next isn't unreasonable, just a narrow alley, not even wide enough for a car. I look to the heavens and beg to fly, ask for the grace to defy gravity for just this moment. These few seconds of hurtling through air, suspended over the certainty of my death, revelling in the value of flight, give me a new sense of freedom, of power over my body, over my fate.

Alone, I can be strong—I can be strong enough. But I need some tools to work with and I seem to have lost them in the long grass. They've been left outside through too many winters, are rusted with the disuse brought about by false comfort. I'm weak, not safe, too vulnerable. I make myself alone and now there's only the music. I float into Satie and Debussy in their quieter moments, but their dissonances always bring me back. I'm in deep waters so I become a diver. I must take time to decompress or suffer the bends. I look for blisters on my emotional heels, damage to my emotional spine. Shaky, but still intact.

I go for a walk in the cemetery. It feels necessary, although I'm not entirely sure why. Intellectually it seems like a morbid thing to do, it should bother me, terrify me, but it doesn't. I look at the names, the dates, the remembrances on the tombstones. For each one I read, that person is remembered, if only in name, for a moment, an instant of acknowledgement, a recognition of vulnerability. Death offers the kind of truth we deny ourselves in life, a soul-to-soul acceptance, a silent greeting. I walk out of the thickly grassed quiet feeling calm.

I spend most of the afternoon in the park. I watch the water of the fountain cycling through and back, and lie in the thick grass willing myself to be absorbed by earth, fall into it. Try for calm, for flow, for rhythm, the refrain from Dylan's "Don't Fall Apart on Me Tonight" cycling through my head.

The morning sky's too blue, too bright. Ascend me to heaven on a morning like this. I can almost feel the cold air punching holes through my body, body freed in the violence of that embrace. Allow me to turn away from this confrontation with slow death and face heaven now, simply.

There's power in the naming of things, a simple magic. Once named, once understood, the power of the object is defeated.

I don't know if I'm ready for this. The two weeks are up. The clinic won't open for another hour. I wait, feel heaviness compressing my lungs, feel like a sailor tied to the mast of time, and look up at the sky. I go to the closet, pull my wallet from my coat pocket, remove the health clinic card from the wallet, all the time moving like a sedated deep-sea diver. There's the need for ritual, the need to dial the number with slow care. The receptionist puts me on hold, unsure if the test results are in. I look out the window to the sky, refuse to feel my body.

She comes back on the line, says "Sorry, they're not back yet." My heart's thumping through the floor. "Oh. Wait a minute. The courier just came in. Can you hold again?" My breath starts coming faster, sweats in and out of my lungs, pulling at blood and muscle deep inside. I shake, hanging on the telephone, eyes closed. *Click* and she's back. "Sorry about that. We have your results." They don't give the results of AIDS tests over the phone, even if the results are negative.

I have to know now. Other people know already: the lab technician, the receptionist, the counsellor. I reach for my Dad's overcoat and crawl inside. I leave the apartment needing to be at the clinic in the next breath. I've never run like this before. I move in a blind panic, chased by demons, breath expels hard, cold air wrenches deep in my lungs. I'm briefly conscious of people on the street turning as the madwoman runs by. Slow down, walk, catch breath out of air, feel blood pumping deep in my ears. Pace myself up that last hill to the clinic, exhausted, shaking, sweating despite the cold. One last look skyward, savouring the light, the air, before I open the door and step into the waiting room.

This is a difficult thing I've come to do and it's most difficult now. I need to be calm, composed. I need to be in total control. I feel the tension in the muscles of my face; it's a serious face, a worried face, a face fighting to maintain composure. There will be no tears. I don't cry in public, I don't make scenes, I don't like to make other people uncomfortable. I close my eyes carefully, slowly. I watch the patterns of the blood moving on the inside of my eyelids.

My heart beats faster, harder than usual. I feel its rhythm rocking my body as it pumps blood through the arteries. There's sweat on the back of my neck and in my clenched hands. Somewhere inside, a shiver I can't quite control. I fight hard against my body's rebellion, swallow hard against a harsh, unwelcome sound threatening to escape.

I will not cry. I'm stronger than that. I have to be. My fist clenches tighter, nails leave marks on my palm, strained knuckles freeze white. I bite the inside of my lip, feel the fang go into flesh, taste dark blood. Pain as control. I inconspicuously brush away the watery salt collecting in my eyes. I will not cry. I will fight for control of this body. I fight for control like a hooked fish.

A young man sits across from me. He seems fragile, ready to break, combust. His face twists into tears and the friend holding his hand reaches an arm around him and leans his worried face close to those tears, holds him and tells him quietly, "We're in this together." The friend notices I'm looking. He gives me one of those waiting-room smiles that says, *We're all frightened. We're all in this together.*

The counsellor calls me into his office. It's a small room, quietly lit and warm like a womb. He closes the door behind me and turns, looks at me. In that look, he penetrates the fragile shell of exterior control, sees through me, knows what contortions I've undergone in the waiting. And my mask crumbles. He waits silently, ready to catch me as I begin my emotional descent. *I will fight for control of this body...* He touches my arm gently, reassuringly, a touch I haven't felt for so long—the touch of another human being. My body shudders. He reaches for me, embraces me. And I'm lost. I cry the tears I've denied myself, finally allow the tears I thought were a sign of weakness, tears I thought would dissolve me. Am crushed in a flow of anguish I can't restrain any longer. Freed. His touch, the warmth of his embrace, is real and human. Everything's going to be all right.

The threat of AIDS is a poor, falsely evaluated reason for continuing in a relationship that's not working. I thought I could maintain a façade in a situation that was emotionally vacant and destructive because at least I knew I was safe, or assumed I was safe, that my partner was as monogamous as I was, was not lying to me. Misplaced trust, misevaluation.

You find a new home for the little dog I bought you, one with a yard and children to play with. You and she buy a new dog, a big, dumb, butch animal, trained to a fine edge of obedience. But you retain the apartment below me.

She gets pregnant. Not exactly planned, at least not on your part. I'm proud of the level of control I can exert over the complexity of my emotions. Fear for the child.

She bounces into where I work with the new baby girl,

all proud and triumphant. And...I really don't care. I want to say, *I hope you'll be very happy together and just fuck off out of my life*, but I'm too civilized.

I run into you on the street. You're talking about buying a house with her for your new family. I ask, "How can you afford that?"

You look at me, smile nasty and say, "We just have to yank her Mama's chain and it's ours." Suddenly nauseous, I excuse myself.

Without warning, she takes the baby and moves to the other side of the country. Abandons you. She got you good—better than I ever could've.

I work out everyday, pull my body back into prime condition listening to Kate Bush's "Rubberband Girl." Take my body back, re-exert control, power over myself. Looking good *is* the best defense. At home in the quiet night I justify myself with Counting Crows' "A Murder of One" and re-balance myself with REM's "Everybody Hurts," and "Steady On" by Shawn Colvin.

I was in town a few years ago and saw you on the street. Despite your queasiness about such things, you'd gotten a tattoo around your bicep. Word was you were seeing some eighteen or nineteen year old and having a hard time of it. Some people completely lose their minds when they turn forty.

In this climate, the sky is crystal clear—digital. Wind comes down the bay cool and direct, moves my breath deeply. I want to capture as much of it as I can, hold it in my lungs, my body. Ocean wind blows down my throat, into my nostrils, with the cold clarity of liquid. When this wind plays, it disrupts, rustles like no other, catches my hair so it snakes Madam Medusa style against the breeze, like an angel released from a Blake piece. As it rushes by my ears, it causes momentary deafness—a hush like the sound of blood in arteries plunging through moist interior cavities, the grunt and suck of flesh.

Cloud, heavy and dark like drowning stones. Wind whips the water, creating swirls of white foam. I'm lost and fragile in this foreboding ocean, but still anchored to my chair. I pull the towel around me against the wind, against the chill. It may rain. There's always water. And then we drown.

The deep-sea anglerfish is named for a fleshy luminescent appendage, an extension of its dorsal fin that acts as a lure to attract prey. The lure is only present on the female of the species. Due to the enormous water pressure at depths of sometimes over thirteen thousand feet, its body tends to be rounded and soft. The anglerfish has very tiny eyes and long sharp fangs. Although fierce in appearance, this fish ranges from only four inches to three feet in length and, due to its lack of pelvic fins, is a feeble swimmer. Its dark colour makes it difficult for potential prey to spot in this depth of water where little light penetrates.

The anglerfish causes bioluminescent bacteria in her lure to light sporadically while she waves it through the water like a beacon, attracting unsuspecting fish. With a distensible jaw and imprecise body shape, she is capable of swallowing prey larger than herself.

The half-inch to two-inch parasitic male attaches himself to the female using his sharp teeth. In time they become permanently fused, the male's blood, oxygen and nutritional needs being supplied solely by the female. Their attachment facilitates breeding in an environment where locating a partner is difficult. Multiple males may attach themselves to a single female. Given the parasitic nature of their codependence, it would follow that if any one of the group became ill or died, it could adversely affect the blood supply of the entire assembly.

The giant squid is the largest known invertebrate on earth. Specimens have been recorded at fifty-seven feet in length, weighing approximately one ton, although many specimens are smaller, and it has been projected that growth could exceed seventy feet in length with a weight of two tons. The giant squid has the largest eyes of any known animal. Eyes as large as a human head better enable it to see in the perpetual darkness of the deep sea. Ichthyologists have theorized that the giant squid may also be able to detect bioluminescence, possibly enabling it to locate prey or mates. When under stress, the squid releases sepia ink into the water. Its red torpedo-shaped body can move with surprising speed using rudimentary jet propulsion, forcing water from the mantle cavity of its body by rapidly bringing its arms together.

The most obvious feature of this creature is its many appendages: giant squids have eight arms, each the diameter of a substantial human thigh and lined with two rows of suckers with toothlike serrations on their circumference. In addition, these creatures have two much longer, narrower tentacles with flattened spatula-like ends. These are lined with four rows of serrated suction rings, the diameter and distribution of which changes along the length of the tentacle. The tentacles are usually held close to the body, but extend with alarming rapidity when prey is near. Prey is grabbed in the tentacles, which pull it closer to the other arms where it is further subdued and pulled toward the sharp beak, a toothed vagina-like structure hidden in the skirt of the arms. The beak rips pieces of flesh from the prey, which are further shredded by the tiny filelike teeth of the radula before being swallowed.

The giant squid feeds primarily on deep-sea fish and

other squids. Its only known predator is the sperm whale. Although similar in length to the giant squid (approximately forty to fifty feet), at thirty to forty tons the sperm whale is a significantly heavier animal. Sperm whale stomachs are frequently found to contain dozens of undigested giant squid beaks.

The female squid is thought to produce over a million miniscule eggs (ovular shaped, less than a millimetre in either direction), amassing them in a single gelatinous blob. Although the actual interaction of mating has never been observed, female specimens have been found with spermatangia, the sacs of the spermatophore, in the tissue surrounding their heads and the base of their arms.

Although the giant squid has accidentally been caught at depths of one to three thousand feet, it is more prevalent in deeper waters (a mile or more) possibly dwelling on the ocean floor. Although attempts have been made, an individual has never been observed in its natural habitat. Much of what is known about this creature and its interactions has been surmised from the examination of dead specimens and lesser relatives. Some schools of thought hold that the giant squid is a reclusive lonely hunter, while others hold that it is a ruthless sea monster, the leviathan or kraken of legend.

six

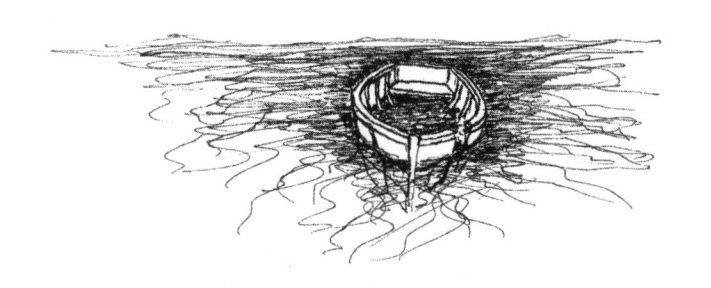

Needing to get away from you, I find another apartment—dark brown interior, north-facing with inadequate heating and insulation. It's such an old building that the toilet is a W.C. separate from the bathtub and sink. The kitchen is a reformed walk-in closet so narrow that the fridge and stove can't be fully opened. The cat spends his days and nights in a depressive sleep. The apartment's only saving grace is its proximity to a twenty-four hour doughnut shop. When I can't sleep, when I wake up at four in the morning, I go and sit and watch the crazies and the drunks and the people with no place left to go, try to figure out what separates me from them.

My neighbours are routinely rousted for drug trafficking and petty theft. Each morning I wake to the sound of a fat mother yelling obscenities at her three timid daughters through the thin wall at the head of my bed. There's noise in the hall, something banging against the walls and floor, shouting. When I peer through the fish eye of my door, another neighbour lies on her back in the hallway, her boyfriend standing above her, booted foot raised over her face.

The anniversary of what would have been my child's birth. I have an emotional crash that lasts for weeks. The impact of the downturn startles me, leaves me second-guessing the decision. But mostly it's the loss, regardless of circumstance, of my child. I need someone to help me through this, but there's no one here. You were the other part of the equation that made this child out of flesh, but you couldn't see how damaged the child would be, couldn't feel the loss the same way. I won't call you. I have to bear this alone. I didn't know, hadn't understood, that it would be like this, that I'd still be dealing with loss a year later, hadn't realized the ramifications, the depth of mourning.

I can only ever count on myself. No one else can be trusted. I must learn to be strong, never to need, never to be vulnerable. I don't want mirrors, can't look at myself, strain for anonymity, for absence. Dark in a room draped with silence, so quiet I can hear the bubbles click against the side of a glass as they escape, detonating into a larger air.

I don't know if I can be naked in bed anymore. I tell myself it's the cold—a bed needs the combined heat of two bodies. I retreat to one side, or even a corner, wear sweats and socks, anything to try to get warm, huddle. Feel cold, lost. But this cold is internal, and no amount of external warmth can remedy it.

Times alone when the shark mind takes a dark bite, when the teeth won't let go until all the juice is sucked out. Tortured response to black holes of absence; sometimes I find a tangible reason—an anniversary, a scar starting to seep—other times it just happens. Darkness takes up all of consciousness, renders me incapable. No appetite, can't force food in, no reason to. Shakes, shivers. Can't get warm. All that reminds me of body is chills. The physical screams for relief while the rest of me ignores it, too intent on pain. Focused on something cold inside, uncoiling in the dark and constricting flow of the rational, the everyday, the insignificant. The body becomes mere surreality. A metallic fever taste in my mouth. Chills. Sounds like flu, only darker, like plague. Only it's all in the head and the heart and the soul. Grieving in fragments of time, suffering attack from requiem sharks.

And there's still no one to share this pain with. That night he and I get too drunk and I talk too much and I tell him, "It's a mistake to cling to anything external from self. Times you most need someone, there isn't anyone there and so you have to find ways of getting by solo."

He struggles with alcohol tears, says, "That's so sad," and looks away.

It's not sad. Just real.

Suicide makes as much sense as not. If I let the blood out of my body, I'll be dead. Simple. The challenge is to find purposes significant enough, weighted enough, to anchor one in life when *not* to be could be so much easier. Of course, the most pleasant prospect would be to be unborn. Not to *be* in the first place.

And then the water, the wanting of water. Dark winter nights crying from some low part of my body. Wracked, wailing of loss, shakes. I curl into fetal position, but then feel that part of my body too exposed, too vulnerable. It's too similar to the position I woke up in after losing my child. Fetal reminding me too much of absence. I try to become fetus, but it hurts. I come back to myself too aware of where flesh has been taken, ripped away, killed. Dare myself to lie flat, stiff, become part of the bed, but the hollow's still there, drawn taught between hips, below rib cage. Bones sharpened by the emotional starvation of loss.

In the cold dark of winter I get up. Heavy, concise, precise efforts to dress in the dark. Move slowly from the bedroom, out of the apartment leaving keys, watch, wallet. Anonymous. Walk in the silent cold dark pre-dawn, cross Water Street at an angle, run the last couple of steps to the other side. It's sometimes windy, always dark and cold, and sometimes starless.

I walk along Parkhill until I make the concrete bridge. Its pillars are crumbling. Halfway across the bridge I stop, place my hands on the cold rail in a carefully measured manner and lean into it for a moment. I stare across the dark night and down to black ice. Swing one leg, then the other up to the concrete railing. I always sit for just another moment looking out at the night. And then I lower myself as far as I can, as gently as I can to black ice. It's not the fall, the flight through air that matters; it's the ice, the ice water, the overcoming black. The ice layer breaks with the contact of my body and I'm through, surrounded by black water, swept under. It's cold under ice, numb, almost silent. Only the sound of water and heart in my ears, the crack and shift of ice. Looking up, it's brighter, so much brighter above me. The ice, jagged and filigreed where I've come through, and then solid, keeping me down. The shock of it wears thin. Cold, numb and black. Peace.

In the calm of this ritual, I can finally go to sleep.

I don't think I'd ever commit suicide as an act of desperation. It just doesn't seem like an appropriate thing to determine on the spur of the moment, is too important, too weighted. This means that if I were to commit suicide, it would be a rational act. I don't see a problem with that. There is no problem with that and that's what scares people—the fact that suicide can be a rational decision, balanced, weighted, decided and acted upon. I perceive death as being not very different from life, only with less flesh and politics.

I couldn't off myself—not yet anyway. I'm not sure there'd be anyone to meet me except maybe a dead baby, but I'm not sure I'd know her if I saw her. Let me be absorbed into the sky on a night like this and follow baby's breath, baby's last breath, homeward.

A silicone heart transplant would alleviate all possible pain. Replace the flesh of that organ with molded pink plastic, the bodily equivalent of a lawn ornament flamingo. Embrace the technology of a new human heart, incapable of emotion, safe.

Waiting for the rain, watching through the strained glass window, I slowly begin to come out of the dark. After jumping into the river I walk along the bottom, still in my clothes. Move slowly, picking through a debris of dead branches—like something out of *The Wizard of Oz*, but not as scary. Like walking down the street, only slower.

I try to turn the page, but it keeps blowing back. And so I carry this little death around with me, a small dark bag, like an old-fashioned doctor's Gladstone. A small, delicate, dangerous piece of luggage I can't seem to lose, can't let go of. I've built a shrine of crucifying guilt from my weakness. Guilt swallows me whole and dark, pulls my guts back to the nerves of my spine. Having acted rationally, having signed once and once only—the power of that. Having signed a piece of paper condoning an act of violence to my body, an order of execution for the one I should've sacrificed my life for. The hollowness, the emptiness, the loss, the physical loss.

In a bookstore I find a volume in my hand about a woman's post-abortion emotional journey. I browse through it, read paragraphs here and there, recognize parts of myself in its passages. Then flip to the end, hoping her conclusion will guide me. She figures that because there are already so many babies in the world, the loss of hers doesn't really matter. I'm angry, unconvinced, slam the book back on the shelf and leave. No individual can replace another.

As I submerge into the underground, a young woman wearing jeans and a sweatshirt stops me with a smile. I smile in return, thinking she's going to ask me for directions, but I'm wrong. Instead she says, "I've just had my fourth abortion." And I feel the hollow in my belly, am aware that something in my face has dropped, but I'm not sure she's detected it. "I've just had my fourth abortion and I'm proud, because now I won't be a single Mom supported by your taxpayer dollars." Amazing the justifications we find to make ourselves feel better.

I have dinner at the Blue Moon. Still looking for answers, finding my way toward a future, I decide to let the palm reader have a look at my hands. She finds traces of the child there, says I will have children. I don't ask, but am sure that what she's reading, seeing there, is the scar of the unborn, the imprint of a life not lived.

By the time you would've been ten years old, I realize my guilt is entirely self-inflicted, self-imposed. You didn't live. It's my fault. I was weak, I let the rational override heart, I made a mistake. I know myself better now. What I learned cost you life. Some days that's sacred, others, it has no value. The decision was made, it's past and I have to live with it. Remove the guilt. The movement of my emotions is of mourning, simple mourning. Take away the guilt, disconnect it, override it, tear it out, and I'm left with simple mourning—and that's enough. Unceasing mourning. The acknowledgement of silent grief. The need to mourn the loss of an intimate. One without a face, without identity.

Awake in the warm night, light from the moon gently fractures on water, breaks on wet rock. And like a three a.m. ocean, I become still. Out there a foghorn blows like a conch shell, sounding gentle and low at a dark distance, no visual contact, a mysterious context. Someone out there is signalling and I can detect the signal, but I don't know how to respond, how to react. I don't know the intention of the sender, if it's *look out, beware, tow me* or *I'm sinking*. The sound, too far out, much further out than I think, gradually fades.

Water slides into sky, merges, becomes one and the same, an all, an entity entirely unborn in a not-time. The invisible thread of the horizontal skyline bleeds into dawn, a glimmer of light starting through cloud. Sun reaches deep from the atmosphere, touches the surface calm, penetrates the ocean, streams through water refracting into lines of pure colour.

The parrotfish is a colourful, large-scaled herbivorous reef dweller. Using its beaklike mouth, it breaks off and eats fragments of coral, spitting out residual sand. Once it has digested its meal of algae and coral polyps, excreted coral skeletal waste helps form white coral sand. It has been estimated that a ton of sand is produced per reef acre, per year, by parrotfish. The sounds of their gnawing transmit through the water, creating a background sound a little like inner-ear crackling experienced during a sinus infection.

Parrotfish are diurnal, sleeping at night in the sand or on the reef bottom. Some species spend half an hour preparing for bed, excreting mucous cocoons that minimize their scent in the water and protect them from nocturnal predators such as eels.

Some species maintain a haremic social structure, with a brighter, larger, primary male heading a school of three or four females. When spawning, the primary male swims in circles around the females. Once a female joins him, the circles become tighter and faster until gametes from both parties are released into the water. The display represents a kind of whirling dervish sexuality. Some species exhibit sexual dimorphism: when the primary male dies, the largest female undergoes a non-surgical sex change, transforming into a supermale. While primary males and females may be a combination of reddish brown and grey, supermales tend to be bright iridescent blue-green with dashes of yellow. However, depending on the species, coloration may change with age, surrounding or gender. These changes, which presumably make sense to the parrotfish, have caused much confusion in attempts to classify these species.

With the aid of stiff pectoral fins and strong lashing movements of its tail, the flying fish can glide through air, staying aloft for as long as twenty seconds, travelling as far as six hundred feet, at heights of up to fifty feet (with a wind) and speeds of over twenty miles an hour. Making six or seven consecutive glides by touching lightly off the water surface with its tail, the fish may be out of water for as long as forty-five seconds and cover a distance of thirteen hundred feet. This behaviour allows the fish to avoid predation from larger, faster-swimming fish. Although it does reduce the chance of predation by other fish, being airborne can lead to predation by ocean birds. When in danger, the flying fish increases water speed using its tail, vibrating it at up to fifty times per second, something approaching the velocity of hummingbird wings. With its winglike fins pressed against its body for streamlining, the fish angles its body toward the surface and rockets out of the water where it spreads its large fins to glide. The pectoral fins can look like gossamer butterfly or fairy wings, or sometimes even resemble feathery bird of paradise wings. In most species only the pectoral fins are enlarged, but some species also have enlarged pelvic fins, providing a four-winged advantage.

A schooling surface dweller, flying fish usually stay in the upper six or seven feet of ocean. Generally about seven to twelve inches in length, some species can range up to eighteen inches. The flying fish is usually dark blue or brown on top and silvery on the bottom. The coloration minimizes visibility to both aerial and ocean predators: birds will have greater difficulty spotting a dark colour against the ocean and fish will have greater difficulty spotting silver against surface light and sky. The large, distinctive eyes of the flying fish are designed to see in both air and water. The enormous eyes also allow it to see its tiny planktonic prey better.

Flying fish spawn near shore in the evenings from spring to summer. The female releases approximately five hundred microscopic eggs into the water. Depending on the species, some eggs float while others sink or become attached to weeds and other surfaces. When hatched about two weeks later, the young bear little resemblance to the adults and have on occasion been mistaken for entirely different species of fish.

Although their flying behaviour is fascinating to watch, it's undertaken out of terror, and the combination of energy expended through panic, takeoff, flight and not being able to breathe while in flight, requires enormous strength. Due to its unusual exertions, the heart of the flying fish is larger than that of other fish its size.

I'm completely bereft of desire. Lost and free falling in limbo, cold air circulating from mind to veins. My fear is that I'm destined to be alone; from that it follows that some things make no difference. At times simplicity is so desirable. But I can't quite...

I want, don't want, can't afford the price. Love is like gambling: if I can't afford to lose, then I'm not going to put my money down. Unfortunately it becomes difficult to conceive of ever winning, of buying into a relationship than can possibly succeed. Heart scrapes like knuckle on stone, like flesh on coral. I've been scraping for a long time and just can't heal.

It doesn't matter how much I may have loved anybody—it's irrelevant. Time and energy wasted and there's no way to recover the loss. I've always had a romantic's idea of love. I expect love to be enough and now I know it isn't, but I still want it to be, feel it should be. And yes, *love is strange* and fickle and seemingly anemic.

I've spent too many years denying my emotional states, smoothing them into hard knots in my stomach, and now the knots are all letting go at once. All the emotions I pretended I didn't have, that I could ignore, that I made go away—didn't. They festered, gnawing and waiting, rotting from the inside, and now picking through this debris of a life to date, I try to figure out if any of it's worth keeping, if any of it's worth anything.

Exertion adds desperation to my confusion; it could be so simple just to be and feel, but I need to quantify, qualify my emotional state into equilibrium. I'm disenchanted by the insatiability of entropy, don't trust that loose feeling in my intestines, must acknowledge my fear of failure.

I disrupt even the simplest of possible conjunctions, jump full throttle to the edge just to make the point that intimate relationships can never work, and so force my own hand into blushing silence and separation, where at least I'm familiar with the parameters.

Sometimes, more subtly, finding a hard clear emotion on the periphery of the zone, I try to creep up to it on my belly. Trench warfare. The emotion retreats as I advance and eventually I lose sight of it. I become a romantic with an edge. Sometimes the emotional knife glints unexpectedly, too uncomfortably close to my throat. But I survive, teetering on the brink of the cliff edge, unsure how to engage.

Nothing is ever completely finished with; scar tissue remains. This weight I carry with me, the last few pounds I never seem to lose—momentarily misplaced perhaps, but never completely lost. The emotional cost weighs heavily, ignored in the daylight, but haunting in dreams, waking with tension in my stomach and jaw. The past is never far enough away. I live a haunted life, have introduced ghosts before understanding the possibility, have not yet found the true way to exorcism.

Inflicted damage has left me weakened when I thought it was making me stronger, tougher. Miscalculation. I don't believe there can be a person who's entirely undamaged. I sustain nothing permanent, but it takes time to appreciate that, cauterize the wounds.

Love is a positive emotion for which I've suffered internal injury too many times. I can no longer say it, think it, without cringing, without apologizing, without praying against experience that *maybe this time,* without short-circuiting any possibility, without shutting it down, without concluding that any given relationship will end disastrously before it's even started. Already anticipating that rivulet ribbon of shock that wafts over me when I know it isn't okay, when I know too late that I'm drowning out of water.

I'm seeking a balance between sensitivity and strength, and trying to determine how pain evolves each factor. On some unexposed level I suspect I'm performing experiments on myself, some twist of Schrödinger's cat in which the observed and the observer are one and the same and quite obviously affect each other. I'm collecting data to be explored at a later date. At some future point I'll be able to divulge the information to myself.

I want to believe fairy tales about romantic love, have had to retrain my naïve self after numerous failures. But fairy tales are seductive; without them there's no blueprint for behaviour or expectation, and I've felt a need for some kind of guidance. If the precedents are abolished, then I don't know where the boundaries are, and so I'm forced to make up the rules as I go along, but nobody's rules are quite the same. What is it we're trying to convince each other of? I live in a society of individuals, but I don't know where that takes me in terms of partnership. Now I'm creating my own code of trial and error, laying bread crumbs in the hope that eventually I'll see a pattern. I become more introverted, become part of the wall, see you through window glass and can't hear you at all.

Male and female. Each of us caught in an awkward genetic endeavour from birth and silence. Perhaps differences in physiology, the tension of addressing otherness, create difficulties in communication. Maybe I could work out a body exchange with a man for a while. It would simply be an effort to discover commonality.

It seems the more experience I have, the more men I know, the more I develop an uncomfortable sense that there are elements inherent in the male psyche that are completely incompatible with who I am, that somehow for me to be in an intimate relationship with a man necessarily entails severely compromising my nature and aspirations. I refuse to do that anymore—not even unintentionally. And that may mean that I am this alone from here on out.

The deep core romantic in me is still trying to hang on and make me believe love is a possible thing, but I fear my ideals may not withstand a further blow. So I stand clear and develop a very active fantasy life, create a delusional world of the romantic love that's all I ever wanted.

Of course, that's the curse of a romantic nature. I become so caught up in possibilities, in the delusion, that sometimes I'm totally incapable of seeing what's actually there, what's actually offered. I'm always wanting what I can't have, but can't trust what's given. And then I start to wonder if I've missed someone already, someone important.

My new apartment is large and bright and clean. The walls are Mediterranean white, my furniture blue, the floor a blond wood. The black cat sleeps on the end of the sofa, the young orange cat at the foot of the bed in a pool of light. The windows face south and let in a lot of sun, even in winter. I don't cover them with blinds or curtains, but let the sun wake me when it does.

I have a dream in which I walk into a sex shop on Queen Street to buy a vibrator. I have another dream in which I have sex with green aliens who come up to my waist. I have to question the state of my romantic being when my sexual dreams no longer contain human referents.

I study the work of artists. Drawings of black-stockinged nudes on account book pages, the curvaceous charcoal lines superimposed, disrupting the symmetry of rule-straight pink and blue columns. Examining Picasso's embraces, rapes, ravishments and strangulations, I'm startled by the sexuality of a few simple lines.

At a photo exhibit, I notice that the images produced by women are more violent than those produced by men. In an erotica bookstore the most openly sado-masochistic work is written by the fairer sex. Maybe it's an attempt at re-asserting power, some strange coercion between dominance and happiness. If all else fails, I'll start taking black-and-white photographs and writing pornography.

The labels we have are for the sullen and the bored. I'd be lying if I said I'd never been attracted to a woman. Especially after that last disastrous split, I never wanted male hands on me again. When she walked through the door at work, her presence stilled me, rendered me breathless. She'd stop by about once a month. Every time I saw her there was a flash of eyes between us—to our mutual embarrassment—but it couldn't be denied. I don't know if she ever told her partner, a woman whose first name she shared. There's something about the red-haired woman that holds my eyes.

This apartment has thinner walls than I'm used to. I awake to the sounds of men next door having sex and hold myself alone in my bed. The black cat moans in sleeping sympathy, adding another male voice. It's four a.m. on the morning of my birthday. I'm surrounded by passionate male sexuality and none of it's directed toward me.

My neighbour and I see each other in the hall, strike up a conversation, become friends. He and I go for brunch and sit on the patio of an intimate restaurant with a high proportion of gay clientele. As I butter my toast, I listen to the conversation of the two men behind me, a discussion about the relative merits of steel versus gold handcuffs.

Then he and I go into a sex shop just for fun. Most of the magazines are hermetically sealed and there's a lack of gadgetry. The most entertaining device is a vibrator with a number of heads that can be interchanged for different effects. He looks at it in dismay, comments on its size and suggests it must be a child's starter model.

He and I watch men pass like we're shopping. He likes physically large men, but I don't. I find them threatening, am always cautious in their presence, aware of the physical damage they could inflict. I prefer smaller men, boyish, with smooth skin taut over vein and muscle and bone. Whenever I express interest in someone on the street, he assures me they're gay.

We can discuss sexuality openly because we both know it's not part of our relationship. In our conversations I can confirm some of my worst suspicions about the nature of masculine desire. He says he can understand the affinity between gay men and straight women—it's the quality of the individual that matters.

I find myself associating with men who are gay and falling for men who are sexually ambivalent, because I can talk to them. They're less sexually accessible and that's just safer.

Another new friend and I go to a drive-in movie, watch something forgettable while lying on a blanket on the hood drinking wine and eating popcorn. It's a dusk to dawn show, but we give up at about two-thirty and drive to the water for a swim. Naked in the dark; cool air and warm shallows caressing. Laughing and playing and touching. Get out shivering, hugging for warmth, amazed by the smoothness of his skin despite the goosebumps. Air cool-drying us as we sit on a log holding hands, waiting for dawn. Mutually stolen gentle kisses on parting, but no more. I want to take it further, but somehow it feels inappropriate to make the first move in this case. I value the friendship too much to risk causing him discomfort and I feel it would have to be his decision. He knows I'm open to the possibility and that's enough.

I have a dream in which I'm cuddling a small black cat—until he turns into a little boy, blond and restless and fragile. He's sleeping in my arms and I cradle him, rest my chin against him. Kiss the top of his head and watch his lashes dance as he dreams.

I try to explain to the restaurant server that I only need one menu as he thrusts two into my hand. I eat dinner alone on a broad open patio that seats two hundred. Just me and the mosquitoes and the odour of bilge water. Something in the heat, breeze, palms rustling, the sheer power and slow intensity of the ocean rush. Words begin to merge with space and blue-green sky intense with tropical sun.

I don't want my whole life to be about loss. Guided by desires, wishing for satiation, I treat myself. Order Killer Chocolate Cake and a bowl of café au lait, savour the last of my wine by dim candlelight.

People arrive. I feel my centre re-emerging by degrees. Fascinating. So many rapid turnarounds I've corkscrewed. Don't know if I've gone clockwise or anti-, don't know if I've buried myself in the ground or taken off into airy space. Never was any good at physics.

Later, after drinking too much with other holidaymakers, the man I've only just met gets up to leave. I stand, thinking we are about to shake hands. He mumbles, "Let's do this right," and moves to hug me, the closest contact I've had with a man for months. There's something sexual in our momentary contact. And it's not so much the hug, but the *hmm* sound he makes, the sigh exuding from him at a physical moment, that kind of deep non-verbal sound that always seems sexual, creates a vague spark, a reverberation through my chest and body, a brief flicker of smile before he stumbles out the door.

Walking home alone, I'm aware of the emptiness of the street. Notice too late the large man stumbling drunk toward me. Suddenly sober, I calculate distance, make myself big, look straight ahead as he looms closer. Past me, I'm aware that he's stopped. Not wanting to turn my head, I strain my eyes searching for peripheral movements, adrenaline getting ready for the sprint. "It's too cold to be out here without a jacket. You should put a jacket on," he slurs and then turns to continue on his way. I almost laugh out loud with relief.

The TV in my room shows a movie trailer that tells me I'm supposed to be looking for my soulmate. No more flashes in the pan. But something worries me—what if my soulmate has already been run over, damaged beyond repair by this life? What if he's a basket case by the time I find him? Women's work is never done.

The force I have to exert to move through water. Something's happening to me, something that's taking the sting out of my cynicism. The end of bitterness. All those times when I felt myself incredibly well adjusted, I was actually deeply embittered. Now I understand that the right partner will cause me to feel creative and centred and strong and balanced, instead of the imbalanced, bankrupted shadow of myself I've hardly recognized at times.

I trip over this life, not quite sure when it started. Not quite sure what my first conscious act was, my first act of rebellion, defiance, my first mistake, injury. Memory's not distant enough, refined enough; the language of its early transcriptions can no longer be understood.

What was lost, what I couldn't see, were the secret things that lay undisclosed. Fermenting for years, they slowly rose to the top like gas bubbles bursting in air, substance to be skimmed off in words, spat out. There are no secrets here—they've all been released into the atmosphere. The only resolution is that there is no resolution—only motion and time. A flash of parrotfish-blue tail breaks the rippled surface. Clean air blows from unforeseen shores bringing an odour of memory that pulls me past mystery and the child to the sea.

A distant boat bell catches the breeze, a subtle, irregular sound guiding me to the wooden wharf, the journey interspersed with houses and cemeteries. A gentle sound as shallow water slaps against frayed wood. Along this beach the only man-made things are squared timbers with rusted spikes protruding, bits of broken ship, heavy metal sheeting bent and boltless, thick with rust. I find a bloodied ivory-handled knife in the sand.

At the windiest, highest point of the cliff face, a plaque is embedded in the rock engraved to "a husband, father, friend" who died at sea a few years ago. A little further along, rests an anchor made of white plastic carnations with the word DAD surrounded by hearts constructed from faded pipe cleaners. People still get lost at sea, are separated from others by ocean.

I watch someone who looks like me snorkelling in the surf, but it's too rough. She keeps swallowing water, coming up panicked, struggling against overwhelming waves. All night I dream I can't escape the stings of jellyfish.

By morning, my dreams have turned to the seahorse, a

tiny, distinctly shaped fish, with a bony armour-plated body, an upright posture with its head at right angles, a crownlike coronet and a prehensile tail. Its eyes can focus together to achieve binocular vision or they can swivel independently. Although it relies on live prey such as brine shrimp, the seahorse is a weak swimmer, unable to take chase. However, it can use its elongated snout to extract small crustaceans from plants or other surfaces. It lives in shallow coastal waters, seagrass pastures, coral reefs or mangrove swamps, and is faithful to one site.

Seahorses form lifelong partnerships. To confirm their bond, the pair performs a ritualistic greeting each morning, entwining each other's tail in a dance before going on their solitary ways to feed for the remainder of the day. When mating, the dance continues for hours as the partners twirl, pivot and rise in the water, changing colours and making distinctive clicking sounds by tossing their heads in a very horselike gesture. The female sprays her already fertilized eggs into the male's brood pouch (located on the underside of the tail) where they gestate for about three weeks. The hatchlings remain sealed in the brood pouch until they are large enough to fend for themselves. When birthing, the male latches onto a plant with his prehensile tail and proceeds to jerk back and forth rapidly, expelling the young from his pouch at brief intervals. Should any unhatched eggs remain in the male's brood sack, they will decay, forming gas, and buoy the male to the surface where he will fall easy prey. Seahorses are slow to recover from the loss of a mate, and should they find a new partner, reproductive output may be lower. Relative to other fish, seahorses have small broods, with the young taking eight months to a year to fully mature. Seahorse populations are threatened by overfishing and loss of habitat.

seven

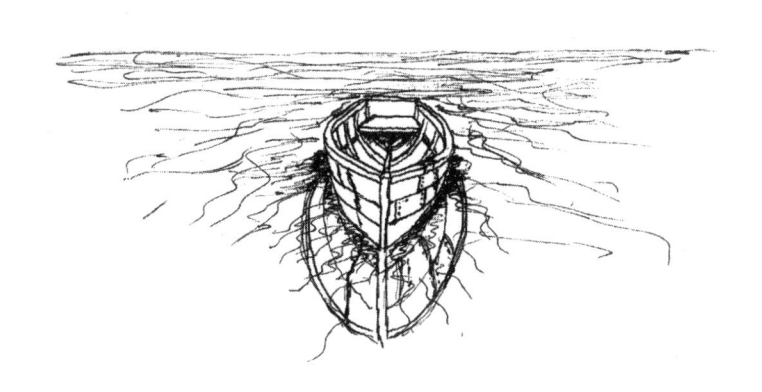

𝓐nd so, this is how I end up here. My body's scarred, but nowhere anyone can see it. Memory is like the ocean: the further into the day, the more animated, complex its surface becomes and the harder it is to see the bottom clearly. I want to go back to that morning calm, but it's too late. Time doesn't run backwards—it always slides toward greater entropy, rougher waves, more whitecaps. All I could do was hope for a lifeline, some piece of flotsam to grab onto, something to get me back to shore safely. And now that I'm on shore, penetrating past, I ponder my desire to get my feet wet again.

Try to calculate what I need to get my life back to zero. Loss doesn't enter into it. There's always loss—it's simply a matter of design. Loss balances gain. Bitterness has faded into an obscure memory of a self I no longer contain. Wonder if my asocial, asexual state will continue, wonder how it adds to the equation, a return to some prenatal state. Sleepy with the warm breeze, the rhythm of the ocean.

I write a postcard to no one in particular. On the front is a bright yellow starfish, radiant with intention. *Intuition is the pre-conscious peripheral vision of the analytical. I may be ceasing the treading of water soon. Anticipating forward motion.*

    Limits shift constantly and so I'm always testing their edges, but at some point I have to ask, whose limits am I testing? Change is like falling off a cliff, but one must endeavour to do so with grace, swallowing any urge to anxiety. I want to be a razor's-edge walker, a cliff-hanger, an entropic terrorist of the self. And so I put my faith in metaphor because straight words fall short. I need courage now. Maybe I'm still too rattled. Maybe the straight line got me, knocked off too many edges. No, but it does keep me back, tries to hold me down, tie me up, make me try to fit some mythical norm. Sometimes I scare myself. I jump at intuition's will, part of me waiting, analyzing. That gap, hesitation between theory and practice, time to second-guess. No wonder I get anxious tension in my gut—waiting for everything else, the analytical, to catch up and react.

    I'm bitten by confusion. Not good. But isn't there always some level of confusion? Some level of insecurity? What if I get slapped down? Try again. I've had bruises and scars before and doubtless will again, but I'm still here. Doubt less. Insecurity. Don't look down; concentrate on the action, not the anxiety. Balance the fears of life, of sanity, of creation—all oppositions understood. The confused cross-sections of love-death, sex-death, lust-love envelops this moment of vulnerability, of cliff-hanging, of nude tightrope walking.

    I don't know if I'm looking particularly hot today or what. An elderly gentleman opens a door for me, a middle-aged man opens a second. Halfway down the block a beautiful younger man—dressed in an open grey trench coat, clean-shaven, dark-eyed—smiles at me. I have to admit I'm feeling pretty buoyant, but I'm also left trying to figure out exactly why I'm evoking these reactions. I'm wearing jeans, a linen jacket—nothing special. But somehow I feel I'm standing taller, straighter, feel less weight on my shoulders. Maybe sex appeal is nothing more than good posture.

At breakfast I actually notice a guy sitting by himself in a booth at the restaurant. I'm ushered past to another booth, one with a kitschy '50s lamp by it. I like this booth, good light for reading. I put the man out of my head.

In the newspaper, there's a cartoon in which the character intones all the ways he wants love, but then declares he's too busy for a relationship. I tear it out to wedge in the upper corner of the mirror in my room. I too keep myself busy—always with important and worthwhile things—but I keep myself busy as a sophisticated form of escape. Busyness is a complex and deceptive form of procrastination, of avoiding dealing with what's really important. I keep myself busy so when I roll into bed at the end of the day, I'm too exhausted to consider how little of the bed I take up, to consider anything other than sleep.

Van Morrison wails "Moondance" in mono as I suck back coffee. The booth is at the back, far away from the sun. I notice myself in the restaurant mirror in a way I usually don't. Maybe I could convince myself that I actually look sexier this morning than I did yesterday, but I can't calculate how much internal shifts show outwardly.

I look up as two guys walk by the restaurant window, both beautiful. Something internal has definitely shifted that I'm even noticing them. The accompanying music wails *Man-sized inside*. Yeah, but a little out of practice too. The spandex nature of human flesh is an asset. Makes me want you. And could I accommodate you both at once? Maybe it's the chocolate talking. Wait—I haven't eaten any. But still, fantasies of a ménage à trois with me at the advantage have been running through my head for years. Just not enough nerve to make it happen. I don't, because that's just pure hormonal, animal instinct. That's just consumption. And I don't want to consume another and I don't want to be consumed myself.

Reading through the paper, I consider running an ad. WANTED: A man who's compassionate, respectful and supportive—but not married. A man who, regardless of age, has already had his mid-life crises, i.e., knows what the hell he's about and how to get there. A man of sound intellect who's not lacking in spirit. A man who's honest, sensitive and highly communicative. A man who can meet me in the middle in oh so many ways. A man who will not only accept me for who I am, but actually encourage me to be myself. A man capable of functioning in everyday practicalities, but not lacking in creative imagination. A man who's beautiful—but not gay (bi is fine—as long as I can watch). A man who's capable of monogamy, or at least capable of not lying about his indiscretions and responsible enough to practise safe sex during sessions of penile wander. A man willing to vocalize his sexual satisfaction openly and honestly. A man who is a sophisticated and inventive lover, willing to experiment. A man who knows when to back off—but who also knows how to hold on. A man who wouldn't usually read, and would never respond to, an ad like this one.

I'm looking for the hand that fits my throat the way the prince looks for the foot that fits the glass slipper. I'm looking for the hand that can be trusted with the musculature, the rings of evenly spaced cartilage, taut but fragile, and be aware of the heavy pulse of my blood. Here, wrap your hand around my throat and I'll tell you if you're the one. But if I back away, remove your hand with a shudder up my spine, you'll just have to accept that it would never work out.

As I'm leaving the restaurant, another guest from my hotel sees me, offers me dinner. I'm still so bad at knowing how to decline politely. We have dinner in a restaurant steeped in that specific blue of a tropical sunset, with a six thousand-gallon aquarium displaying only two fish and a solo musical act playing a mix of seventies rock and Harry Belafonte tunes. The meal is spiced with good conversation and I'm actually glad I've accepted. Toward the end of dinner he stops and looks at me intently for a moment before saying, "I find you really attractive." I duck my head, flush with embarrassment, react the same way I did when I was twelve. I sometimes think of the appropriate response later, the response that would have come from the mouth of Lauren Bacall or Marlene Deitrich. But those lines were always scripted. In the moment, I always fumble. I thank him, apologize that it isn't mutual, pay my half of the tab and walk myself back to my room.

This ocean frightens me with its power, its abandon, its depth. I approach respectfully, knowing it has the power to overcome me. But what happens if I let it, stop resisting? Let the waters swell until they knock me off my feet. Let go of the sterile safety of the shoreline where I can see all the dangers, but from a safe distance. Where I can nurse these scars, tend them, remember them, nurture them, but not allow the possibility of collecting new ones. And what of the desirable, passionate things? A touch, skin, a kiss, a soft murmur, a moan. The light of soft morning catching a lover asleep beside me. A simple embrace.

There's a rhythm here, like breathing. Relationships are never always on the inhale, the exhilaration of the heady, the hyperventalative. Sometimes one must exhale, create distance, re-centre the self, disengage, but not walk away. Just ponder and wait for the next intake of breath, re-oxygenate, find love again.

In the dream I'm in the ocean swimming among many boats and getting caught in their fishing lines. I'm called in from shore. I go inside for lunch and announce to my Dad that I'm going to retire to the British Virgin Islands and buy a yacht. He says, "Okay. Let me make a note of that," and pulls out a large-format book on retirement and starts looking through the index for articles on boats. We debate whether I should go for a twenty-five or a forty footer. In my mind, in the dream, I wonder if this is what I really want—to live on a boat—or whether I just want to be by the ocean, buy a beach house somewhere. I don't know. Things always come into focus the closer they get; whether spatially or temporally, it's the same thing.

I'm suffering like a fish out of water who can still hear the surf. I get up from my chair and look out at the waves, their motion leading me forward. I can see gradations of colour, can see shapes in the water, but I can't identify what they are, whether they're dangerous or beautiful or both. I test the water. A comforting coolness, its salt resisting my penetration. The water gently caresses my toes, my foot, and then recedes with each wave. I'm tempted, but not ready yet. I turn away from the ocean and walk back to my chair to watch for a while longer.

From here I can see the house that's slowly sinking, becoming one with the ocean. It once belonged to a sea captain who didn't want to be too far from the water and so he built right on the stony shore with the front steps descending into the waves. The heavy stone house resisted tides and winds, but as it settled, it slowly dropped closer and closer to the ocean. Now the water licks the front steps even at low tide and visitors are obliged to use the back door.

I sometimes open my eyes underwater in dreams. In the dream I'm swimming in the China Sea. I'm with someone, but I don't know who. The water's brown and thick. It's hard to swim. In the ocean there are jellyfish, sharks, small sparks of life. There's a dare in that. The facing of unseen dangers, but with the knowledge they may never attack.

Globally, about ten people die annually from shark attacks, while in the same period humans kill in the neighbourhood of seventy million to two hundred million sharks. Even in waters heavily populated by sharks, the possibility of death by drowning is still over ninety times greater than that of death by shark.

Strange how moments change, one to the next. I just got some part of my self back. Something small and intangible clicked into present place. I want to make my life the way it is in my head, achieve that slow act of becoming. We build ourselves, construct ourselves, grasping for our own reality. I spent my twenties thinking, *I'll be dead soon*, and it took until thirty to understand that I'm just beginning. And that's not to make me lazy—it's to make me calm.

I've had a series of dreams each successive night for the last several days. Dreams about men I've known. Gentle touches and looks, but not sex. The sex is somehow beyond what we're doing, not part of the picture. But we're often skin on skin and naked and touching. Men I've known and maybe would've been good with, but it just didn't work out, relationships not quite fully explored. My mind is trying to supply me with something, point to something, lead me to what's been missing. As capable as I am functioning as a solo project, there is somehow something desirable lacking, a lack of hands and skin, a lack of contact, of intimacy.

I'm submerging and emerging at the same time, turning myself inside out. The dichotomy of ocean water—it's wet but it dries. Or the contradiction that the sun both bleaches and tans.

Emotion is the texture of existence. I keep checking my heart elevations: calm, beating about ten times per wave, intense as always. And I send another postcard addressed to no one in particular, unaddressed like a message in a bottle. It's a photo of a deserted beach and on the back I write, *I am naked and wet. Wish you were here.*

The ocean just goes. It starts here, where I am, at the shore, and just goes, its surface shattered into fragments of glaring lights and variegated shadows to beyond where I can see, where the world ends, drops off the horizon. Whitecaps white-topped with foam, frothed by wind, and as the water leaves the shore, sliding back into the body of its volume, there's still a little white foam on top like diminished latte.

I imagine that with measured effort I could make my way out to the impossible Sargasso Sea and float where the water's clear, still, warm and safe. The mat of lush green-brown vegetation on the surface masks a desert below where few dangers lurk. I'll make my home in the sun with juvenile butterfly fish, marlin, flying fish and sea turtles. Allow myself to be nurtured. The Sargasso is where the ocean is most still, where ships used to become becalmed and were forced to dump their live cargo of horses overboard. Five thousand to twenty-three thousand feet below me are the skeletons of Spanish horses, reincarnated now into seahorses. Mammals don't do well here in the horse latitudes where the water moves too slowly, meditatively, takes three years to circulate its full clockwise course. Becalmed, be calm. But I may have to work my way through some sharks to get there.

I undress slowly in the still early morning, place my clothes carefully under sandals so the wind doesn't catch them. Feel the ranging textures of sand and coral and vegetation under my bare feet as I move down the beach, closer to the blurred line where land and ocean meet. Gentle waves push sand across my toes, my feet slowly buried. I take tentative steps forward, water lapping higher against my legs. Stand breathing clear light, body swaying with the thrust of each wave. Prepare with one last breath and let myself fall into the water. Cold opens my skin, slaps me alert, clears my vision, moves under my arms, through my hair, between my legs. Pervasive. Opens me, travels through me. I lie just below the surface and watch bubbles travel, ride to light, to air, and then follow them, bursting and elated.

And then I'm swimming in the ocean.

Acknowledgements

A special thanks to Elisabeth Mann Borgese for her kindnesses during my trips to Nova Scotia, and to Paul McConnell and Trudi Seaberg for their hospitality during my trips to the British Virgin Islands. Some of the ocean in this book was derived from personal observation, experience and photographs during trips to Canada's east coast and the Caribbean. Visual stimulation was also gained from the amazing underwater photography of Norbert Wu and David Doubilet. Detailed information on marine life was gleaned from a variety of on-line sources, most notably: the Encyclopedia Britannica; The University of Michigan's Animal Diversity Web, a site that contains a great deal of well-organized information about a variety of wildlife; the Smithsonian Institution's Ocean Planet exhibition, especially useful for information on the giant squid; Nova on-line, especially for detailed information on seahorses; Whitman College's Deep-Sea pages which contain research and photos of a variety of abyssal fish; Canadian Shark Research Laboratory, especially with regard to shark reproduction; Discovery on-line; the International Shark Attack File; and the Project Seahorse site, which contains extensive information on the species and threats to it. Although I have endeavoured to write the passages describing marine life with as much accuracy as possible, I'm not an ichthyologist and I apologize for any errors.

DATE DUE
DATE DE RETOUR

MAR 2 7 2004	
MAR 2 3 2004	

CARR McLEAN   38-296